Wildfire Island Docs

Welcome to Paradise!

Meet the small but dedicated team of medics
who service the remote Pacific Wildfire Island.

In this idyllic setting relationships are rekindled,
passions are stirred, and bonds that will last a
lifetime are forged in the tropical heat…

But there's also a darker side to paradise—secrets,
lies and greed amidst the Lockhart family threaten
the community, and the team find themselves
fighting to save more than the lives of their patients.
They must band together to fight for the future
of the island they've all come to call home!

Read Caroline and Keanu's story in
The Man She Could Never Forget
by Meredith Webber

Read Anna and Luke's story in
The Nurse Who Stole His Heart
by Alison Roberts

And watch for more
fabulous *Wildfire Island Docs* stories
coming soon from Mills & Boon Medical Romance!

Dear Reader,

If you were asked to think of the most romantic setting ever, where would it be? A candlelit dinner? A walk in a forest with dappled sunlight filtering through the canopy? In front of a crackling fire on a winter's night? Or maybe a beach on a tropical island—at sunset?

Those all work for me, that's for sure, but there's obviously something about the tropical island beach that puts it closer to the top of the list for many people—which probably explains why travel agents use those stunning images of couples on beaches to advertise islands.

I've been lucky enough to visit Hawaii, Fiji and Samoa. I'm also lucky enough to have writer friends who love island settings for romantic stories as much as I do, so when the opportunity came up to work together we were all excited.

Wildfire Island is the star of our fictitious archipelago of M'Langi. It has a beach that is so famous for its amazing sunsets it gave the island its name. It also has a hospital, and a team of people who all have their own stories.

This is Luke and Anahera's story. They've both kept huge secrets from each other and have to deal with the repercussions of having them revealed. What are those secrets and how do they do that?

Read on and find out…

With love,

Alison xxx

THE NURSE WHO STOLE HIS HEART

BY
ALISON ROBERTS

First published in Great Britain 2016
By Mills & Boon, an imprint of HarperCollins*Publishers*
1 London Bridge Street, London, SE1 9GF

ISBN: 978-0-263-26367-1

Our policy is to use papers that are natural, renewable and recyclable
products and made from wood grown in sustainable forests. The logging
and manufacturing processes conform to the legal environmental
regulations of the country of origin.

Printed and bound in Great Britain
by CPI Antony Rowe, Chippenham, Wiltshire

Alison Roberts is a New Zealander, currently lucky enough to live near a beautiful beach in Auckland. She is also lucky enough to write for both the Mills & Boon Romance and Medical Romance lines. A primary school teacher in a former life, she is also a qualified paramedic. She loves to travel and dance, drink champagne, and spend time with her daughter and her friends.

Books by Alison Roberts

Mills & Boon Medical Romance

The Honourable Maverick
Sydney Harbour Hospital: Zoe's Baby
Falling for Her Impossible Boss
The Legendary Playboy Surgeon
St Piran's: The Wedding
Maybe This Christmas…?
NYC Angels: An Explosive Reunion
Always the Hero
From Venice with Love
200 Harley Street: The Proud Italian
A Little Christmas Magic
Always the Midwife
Daredevil, Doctor…Husband?

Visit the Author Profile page at millsandboon.co.uk for more titles.

For Meredith and Linda with very much love xxx

CHAPTER ONE

STEPPING OFF A plane could be more than stepping onto unfamiliar ground.

Sometimes it was like stepping back in time.

The heat of the early evening was the first thing that Luke Wilson noticed. The kind of heat laced with moisture that felt like the anteroom of a sauna. Why on earth had he chosen to fly in a suit?

Because that was what internationally renowned specialists in tropical diseases wore when they were invited to be a keynote speaker at an exclusive conference?

The smell was the second thing that hit Luke as he walked from the plane towards the golf cart that was clearly waiting to transport him to his accommodation at Wildfire Island's newest facility—a state-of-the-art conference centre.

He'd already shed his jacket on the small private plane that he'd boarded in Auckland, New Zealand—the last leg of a very long journey from London. Now he loosened his tie and rolled up his shirtsleeves as he breathed in the scent of fragrant blossoms like frangipani and jasmine being carried on a gentle, tropical breeze.

And it was the smell that did it.

It smelled like…

Oh, man…it smelled like Ana.

The emotional reaction slammed into him with far more force than he had anticipated. A mix of guilt. And loss. And a longing that was still powerful enough—even after so many years—to make him wonder if his knees were in danger of buckling.

He shouldn't have come back here.

'Let me take that for you, Dr Wilson.' The smiling young island lad held out a hand to take his small suitcase. 'Hop on board and I'll take you to your bure. You've got just enough time to freshen up before the cocktail party.'

Cocktail party? For a moment, Luke hesitated— his brain fuzzy from a mixture of displacement and the opposing time zone. Oh, yes…this was the 'meet and greet' session before this exclusive conference started tomorrow. A chance to reconnect with his esteemed colleagues from all over the globe who shared his passion—the ambition to make a real difference in the world. Harry would be there, too, of course. More formally known as Sheikh Rahman al-Taraq, Harry was a patient turned friend who was bringing that ambition close enough to touch…

Luke's suitcase was strapped onto the back of the cart and the young man was giving him a curious look, clearly aware of his hesitation.

'You ready, Dr Wilson?'

Luke gave a single, curt nod, defying jet lag as he focussed on what lay ahead for the next couple of days. The nod dispelled any ghosts as well. Anahera didn't live here now. She'd moved to Brisbane almost as soon as he'd left Wildfire Island nearly five years ago. The weird sensation—a curious mix of opposite ends of the spectrum between dread and hope—was nothing more than a waste of mental energy.

'I'm ready.' He climbed onto the cart, smiling at his chauffeur.

'I just don't get it.' Sam Taylor, one of the permanent doctors at Wildfire Island's small hospital, shook his head as he stirred his coffee. 'All the comings and goings and the research centre being fenced off for so long. Now we have private jets coming in and it seems that we have a boutique international conference venue on Wildfire Island. Why here?'

Anahera Kopu shrugged. 'It's a gorgeous place. Different. Exotic enough to attract people who might need an inspiring break as a background to sharing knowledge and doing the kind of networking that's important in the scientific world.'

'I get that. But I still don't understand why someone would choose a place as exotic as the M'Langi Islands. How did they even know about us? And can you imagine how much it has cost? Who's behind it and why has it been such a secret?'

Anahera shook her head. 'I have no idea. But it's not the only secret on this island, is it?'

Oh, help…what an idiotic thing for her—of all people—to say. She had been keeping something huge a secret from all the people who meant the most to her—her mother and her colleagues and friends who were her wider family.

Sam grinned. 'Do tell, Ana…you must know a few more than me. You grew up here and I'm just a newbie.'

Anahera kept her tone light enough to make the conversation impersonal. She'd had plenty of practice at steering conversations in a safe direction.

'No, you're not. You've been here for years now.' She turned on the hot tap and reached for some dish-washing liquid. 'You arrived just after I went off to Brisbane to do my postgrad training, didn't you?'

'Mmm…when the research station was just that. A research station. Now we find out it's been added to and turned into some exclusive resort that's going to be used for medical think tanks and—not only that—there's a rumour that apparently there's been some amazing breakthrough that's going to be announced. Something that could change our lives. Don't you think someone might have told us about that? What do you think it is?'

'No idea. Unless they've come up with a new vaccine, maybe?'

'Doubt it. That takes years and years and more money than anyone would want to throw at an isolated group of Pacific islands. I reckon it's got something to do with that M'Langi tea they make and how it seems to protect some islanders from encephalitis. Did you know that research started on that decades ago?'

Oh, yes…Anahera had known about that. Not that she was about to share any details. She didn't want to think about it, let alone tell someone else. Unbidden, a memory surfaced of sitting in a swinging chair as a tropical twilight morphed into night. Of arms—heavy but so welcome—resting on her body as she lay back against the chest of the man who was telling about his curiosity regarding the tea. She shook the memory off with a head shake that was visible but fortunately appropriate to a dismissive comment.

'I think they'd decided that the only benefit of the tea was some sort of natural insect repellent so that mosquito bites were less likely and therefore people were less likely to contract encephalitis from them. It's hardly going to change our lives.'

Sam sat down at the table. 'I guess not. What we really need is for the aerial spraying to happen to control the mosquito problem. I wonder if anyone's managed to get in touch with Ian Lockhart yet. He's the person who should be organising it.'

Anahera shrugged. 'Not that I know of. He seems to have fallen off the face of the earth. I wouldn't be surprised to hear he's in Vegas, gambling away any recent profits from the mine.'

'If it doesn't happen soon, we could be in for a few nasty cases this year. We don't want another Hami, do we?'

'Heavens, no.' Anahera could feel her face scrunching into lines of distress. She would be in tears in no time if they started talking about the little boy they had lost to encephalitis a couple of years ago. It had been the most heart-wrenching case of her nursing career so far. Almost unbearable, because the little boy had been the same age as her own daughter.

'Maybe we'll find out at this cocktail party. You all set, Ana? Got a pretty dress?'

'I'm not going.'

'But you're invited. We all are.'

'Doesn't mean I have to go. I want to spend some time with Hana. I haven't seen her all day.' Anahera dried the mug and put it back in the cupboard.

'Bring her, too.'

She laughed. 'Take a three-year-old to a cocktail party? I don't think so… Besides, I said I might stay on till ten p.m. if Hettie decides she wants to go before taking over the night shift.'

Anahera could feel a faint flush of warmth in her cheeks as the quirk of Sam's eyebrow made her realise that she had just pulled the rug out from beneath her excuse of wanting to spend more time with her daughter.

'I just don't feel like being social, okay? I had enough of that kind of thing in Brisbane. Not my scene.'

'There'll be interesting people to talk to who'll only be here for a couple of days. Experts on things like dengue fever and encephalitis. I'm looking forward to hearing what the latest research is all about and any improvements to treatment, never mind what the secret announcement is.'

'And I'll look forward to you telling me all about it tomorrow.' Anahera's tone was firm. Clipped, even. She didn't want to hear people talking about research into tropical diseases. It was too much of a reminder of conversations long past. Like the ones about the M'Langi tea. And the dreams of someone who had planned to change the world for the better. She'd bought into those dreams a hundred per cent, hadn't she? Because she'd been going to be by his side while he made them happen. Even now, that sense of loss could tighten her throat and generate that unpleasant prickle behind her eyes.

'There's going to be a *hangi*. You love *hangis*.'

'I know. Mum's in charge of it, which is why she's

left us to sort the patients' meals tonight.' A quick glance at her watch and Anahera had the perfect excuse to leave. 'I'd better go and get on with the observations and medications round so I can feed everyone before they want to go to sleep.'

Sam shook his head, clearly giving up. 'I'll help with the obs and do the meds. We've only got a few inpatients so it won't take long. Then I'll have a shower and get spruced up while you're playing chef.'

The shower was exactly what he'd needed to clear the jet lag and sensation of displacement but, if anything, it only added to Luke's amazement.

Like the rest of this luxurious bure tucked into the tropical jungle edging the beach, this bathroom could have been plucked from a five-star resort. The walls were an almost flat jigsaw of boulder-sized stones and the floor a mosaic of grey pebbles inset with white ones that made a tribal design of a large fish. The soap was faintly scented with something that smelled like the island—jasmine, maybe—and the towels were fluffy and soft.

Wrapping one of those towels around his waist, Luke stepped back into the round sleeping area where the mosquito nets, still tied back over the huge bed, rippled gently in the sea breeze coming through the louvered windows. He could hear voices outside. People greeting each other as they made their way from the other bures to the meeting hall where the cocktail party would probably be under way already.

None of these dwellings had been here the last time. There'd been a rustic cabin or two that had been used by visiting marine scientists but they'd been closer to the laboratories and had clearly been demolished to make way for the new meeting hall. Luke had never needed to use one anyway. He'd come here to work at the hospital as part of his specialist training in tropical diseases so he'd stayed in one of the cabins set up for the FIFO—Fly-In-Fly-Out—staff that provided medical cover and a helicopter service for the whole group of islands and managed to keep a surprisingly excellent, if small, hospital running.

Even the local people who helped staff the hospital had been excellently trained. Like the nurses.

Like Ana…

Luke pulled on a short-sleeved, open-necked shirt and a pair of light chinos. He combed his hair but decided not to bother eliminating his five o'clock shadow. This evening, in particular, was a gathering of people who knew each other well and they'd been invited to relax here. For the next couple of days the intention was for them to enjoy a tropical break while they shared new ideas and then brainstormed the best way to use this facility in the future.

Outside, the sun was already low and the heavy fragrance of the lush ginger plants screening his bure from the next one made Luke draw in a deep breath. He'd only taken a couple of steps before he turned back, however. How ironic would it be to come here and end up as a patient? Digging into his bag, he found the tropical-strength insect repellent he'd brought and gave himself a quick spritz. He slipped the slim aerosol can into his shirt pocket to take with him in case one of his colleagues had not been so well prepared.

Like the accommodation bures, the meeting hall

had been designed to blend with island style. It had a thatched roof and was open on all sides with polished wooden benches and woven mats on the floor. A table had been set up as a bar, and a man peeled away from the group gathered in front of it.

'Luke. It's so good to see you.'

'Harry.' Luke took the outstretched hand but the greeting turned into more of a hug than a handshake. They were far more than colleagues, thanks to what they'd gone through together years ago. 'I can't believe what you've achieved here.'

'It was your idea.'

'Hardly. I suggested using the laboratories as a base to attract new research. I didn't expect you to run with it to the extent of creating the world's most desirable conference venue.' Luke shook his head. 'You don't do things by halves, do you, Harry?'

'I needed a new direction. Or maybe a distraction.'

Luke's gaze dropped to his friend's hand. 'How is it?'

'Oh, you know…I won't be stepping back into an operating theatre any time soon.' Harry turned away with a smile. 'Let me get you a nice cold beer. Unless you'd prefer something else? A cocktail, perhaps?'

'A beer would be great. But don't worry. I'll get it myself. And I need to say hello to people.' Luke followed Harry towards the bar but got sidetracked on the way when he noticed an acquaintance. 'Charles… it's been far too long. How are things going in Washington, DC?'

'It was snowing when I left.' Charles—an American expert on dengue fever—grinned broadly as he gestured towards their stunning view of the beaches and sea beyond the jungle. 'Have to say, this is a bit of a treat.'

'It's a great place. If you walk past the rock fall at the end of the beach in front of the bures you'll get to Sunset Beach. On an evening like this the cliffs light up like they're on fire. That's how this island got its name.'

'Is that so? You've obviously done your homework.'

'Not exactly. I've been here before. When I was starting my specialty training in tropical diseases I came out to do a stint at the hospital here.'

A short stay that had only been intended to enhance his training but which had ended up changing his life.

Haunting him...

He'd known he would encounter ghosts here but they were so much more powerful than he had anticipated. He should have made it impossible for Harry to persuade him to return but how could he have missed this inaugural event when he'd been present at the moment the dream had started? When he'd been the one to suggest the setting?

'I heard about the hospital.' A tall, blonde woman with a Scandinavian accent had joined them. 'Is it usual for such an isolated group of islands to have such a well-equipped medical centre?'

'Not at all. It's thanks to the Lockhart family that it came about. They discovered the gold and started the mine and the research station.'

'And the mine did well enough to pay for setting up the hospital?'

'Not exactly.'

Another ghost appeared because it was impossible not to remember when he'd first heard this story himself. He'd been walking hand in hand with Anahera, on their way to the best seat in the house for the dramatic show that nature put on every evening at Sunset Beach. He could actually hear the sad notes in her voice as she'd filled him in on a bit of island history.

'It was a family tragedy that made it happen. A premature birth of twins that led to the death of their mother and one of the twins being severely disabled. Their father—Max Lockhart—devoted his life to making sure such a thing would never happen again. He studied medicine himself, lobbied the Australian government for funding and encouraged local people to get trained. I believe he even paid for some of that training out of his own pocket.'

'Amazing…' Charles murmured. 'And now he's set up this conference centre? He's a man with vision, that's for sure.'

'Someone else had this vision.' Luke looked up to smile in Harry's direction. He was outside now, with a group of islanders, and they were taking the top layer off a cooking pit. Steam billowed out and a delicious smell wafted in through the open walls of the meeting house. 'Have you met Sheikh Rahman al-Taraq?'

'I heard a lot about him when I made enquiries after getting the invitation for this meeting. A surgeon, yes? Isn't he funding some extensive research into vaccines for encephalitis? How come a surgeon got so interested in a tropical disease?'

'You'll have to ask him about that.'

'I'll do that. Maybe over dinner. Whatever it is they're dishing up out there smells fantastic. I'm starving…'

* * *

'I don't like fish pie.'

'There'll be some ice cream later, Raoul. As long as you eat your veggies.' Anahera tried to sound firm but she was smiling as she delivered her last dinner tray. 'You won't be eating hospital food for much longer anyway. Didn't I hear Dr Sam say you might be able to go home tomorrow?'

'He's going to see how well I go on the crutches. And talk to my mum about getting to clinics to get my bandages changed.'

'Yes…you've got to keep that leg clean. You don't want to have to have any more operations.'

'I'm going to have a big hole in my leg where the ulcer was, aren't I?'

'Not a hole, exactly, but it will be a big scar and a dent where there isn't so much muscle. And you're going to have to work on building up your other leg muscles with the exercises we've taught you. You've been in bed for a long time.'

'Ana…'

She turned swiftly at the urgent tone of the call to see Sam in the doorway of the two-bed ward.

'Sam… I thought you were at the cocktail party.'

'I was on my way. Got a call. You *have* to come with me.'

Anahera tucked back a stray tress of long dark hair that was escaping the knot on the back of her head. She glanced down at her uniform of the green tunic and three-quarter-length pants that were looking a bit worse for a long day's wear and she shook her head, but Sam was already turning. His voice got fainter as he headed towards their small theatre suite.

'*Now*, Ana. It's an emergency.'

Any thoughts of how she must look vanished as Anahera ran after Sam. He was lifting the heavy life pack in one hand and reaching for an oxygen cylinder with the other.

'What's happened?'

'Could be a heart attack. One of the visiting doctors. Ten out of ten chest pain and nausea. Grab the resus kit and let's go.'

Manu, the hospital porter, had a golf cart already running outside the door.

'Maybe I should stay,' Anahera said. 'We can't leave the hospital unattended.'

'I'll stay,' Manu told them. 'And Hettie's on her way.'

'I need you,' Sam said as he stowed the gear on the back of the vehicle. 'You're the one with the intensive care training. If we have to intubate and ventilate, I want you helping.'

Ana climbed onto the cart. Sam was right. This was exactly the sort of scenario she had covered with her extensive postgraduate training. She could deal with something like this without a doctor around, if necessary, and the opportunity to keep her skills fresh didn't happen that often.

They bounced down the track as Sam opened the throttle. It wasn't that far to the new development but it was far enough to have Anahera running through all the possibilities in her head. Would they find their patient in a cardiac arrest? At least there were plenty of doctors there who could provide good-quality CPR but they would need the defibrillator to have any hope of starting a heart again.

It was almost an anticlimax to rush in and find nothing dramatic happening. A group of people were standing quietly beside a table covered with abandoned plates of food. A middle-aged man was sitting on the floor, propped up by a large cushion. Another man was crouched beside him with a hand on his wrist, taking his pulse. The woman standing beside them, directing a breeze from a fan to the patient's face, was Anahera's mother, Vailea Kopu, who was the first to spot their arrival.

'They're here,' she said. 'You're going to be fine, Dr Ainsley.'

'I'm fine already,' the man grumbled. 'I keep telling you, it's only indigestion. I ate your wonderful food too fast, that's all.'

Sam crouched beside the man. 'Let's check you out to make sure. I'm Sam Taylor, one of the resident doctors here.'

'This is Charles Ainsley.' The man monitoring the condition of their patient turned to look at Sam. 'He's sixty-three and has a bit of a cardiac history...'

Anahera wasn't hearing any of their patient's history. Her hands were shaking as she opened the pockets of the life pack and pulled out the leads they would need to do a twelve-lead ECG and check whether the heart's blood supply was compromised.

She couldn't look up but she didn't need to.

She would have known that voice anywhere...

How on earth had the possibility of Luke Wilson attending this elite conference not occurred to her?

But it had, hadn't it? She'd been avoiding any mention of the upcoming event because that thought had been haunting her. Not attending the cocktail party because she didn't want to hear people talking about research into tropical diseases had been a blanket denial. There was only one person she would really dread listening to. Or meeting. The visiting medical specialists would only be here for a couple of days, she had told herself. It would be easy to stay out of the way.

Much easier not to even know whether Luke was present.

She'd been right to dread this. Even the sound of his voice was overwhelming enough to have her whole body trembling. What would happen if she looked up and made eye contact?

He was still talking to Sam. '...Stable angina but he's due for a coronary angiogram next month.'

'Let's get an ECG,' Sam said. 'Have you had any aspirin today, Charles? Used your GTN spray?'

'I took an extra aspirin for the flight. Forgot my spray.'

'No problem.' Having unbuttoned the shirt, Sam reached for the leads that Anahera had attached sticky dots to. 'Grab the GTN, Ana. And let's get some oxygen on, too.'

Ana...

Her name seemed to hang in the air. Had Luke heard? Or had he recognised her already and was trying to ignore her presence?

Dammit...her hand was still shaking as she pulled the lid from the small spray pump canister.

'Open your mouth for me,' she directed. 'And lift your tongue...'

'I can do that.' A hand closed over hers to remove the canister and there was no help for it—she *had* to look up.

And Luke was looking right back at her.

For a heartbeat nothing else existed as those hazel-green eyes captured her own with even more effect than the touch of his hand had—and that had been disturbing enough.

Her body froze, and she couldn't breathe. Her mind froze as it was flooded with emotions that she'd thought she would never experience again. The love she had felt for this man. The unbearable pain of his betrayal.

And then something else made those memories evaporate as instantly as they'd appeared.

Fear...

This wasn't supposed to be happening. It was dangerous. She had to protect more than her own heart and that meant she had to find the strength to deal with this and make sure nothing was allowed to change.

Determination gave her focus and an unexpected but very welcome sense of calm. It was Anahera who broke the eye contact and found that both her voice and her hands had stopped shaking.

'Fine. I'll put the oxygen on.'

The moment had mercifully been brief enough for no one else to have noticed. Or maybe it hadn't. Sam looked up after sticking the final electrode into place.

'This is Anahera,' he told Luke. 'Our specialty nurse.'

'Yes.' Luke pressed the button on the canister to direct a second spray under their patient's tongue. 'We've met before.'

'Of course...' Vailea was still standing beside them, providing a cool breeze from the palm-frond fan. 'I knew I'd seen you before. You came here to work in the hospital a few years ago.'

'I did.'

'You had to rush away, though… Your wife was ill?'

Oh… God… There it was again. The pain…

'Yes.' The monosyllable was curt. Grudging. Maybe Luke didn't want to remember the way they'd parted any more than she did.

The only blessing right now was that there were only two people in this room who knew what had happened during the few weeks that Luke had been here and only one who knew what the aftermath had been.

Anahera just had to make sure that it stayed that way.

Ana…

Hearing that name had been a bombshell Luke hadn't been expecting.

Oh, he'd seen the green uniform that looked a bit like a set of scrubs from the corner of his eye and had realised the attending doctor had brought an assistant to help carry all the medical gear, but he'd been so focussed on relaying all the information he'd gathered about Charles that he hadn't looked properly.

And then he'd heard her name. Had seen the way her hand had been shaking as she'd struggled to get the cap off the GTN spray pump. It had been an unconscious reaction to take the canister from her hand. Ana had been struggling and he could help. The consequence of touching her hadn't entered his thoughts at all so no wonder it had been another bombshell.

But both of those shocks—hearing her name and

touching her skin—were nothing compared to looking into her eyes for the first time in nearly five years.

How could that be so powerful?

They were just a pair of brown eyes and he must
have met hundreds of people with that eye colour over
those years. How could a single glance into this particular pair make him feel like the ground beneath him
had just opened into a yawning chasm?

It was like the difference between putting a plug
into an electrical socket and somehow sticking your
finger in to access the current directly.

And Ana had felt it, too. He'd seen the shock in her
eyes but then he'd seen something he'd never expected
to see. Something that squeezed the air out of his chest
to leave a vacuum that felt physically painful.

He'd seen *fear*, he was sure of it.

'It's gone.' The voice of their patient sounded ab-
surdly cheerful. 'The pain's completely gone.'

No. Luke rocked back on his heels, his gaze seek-
ing Ana's again.

Charles might well be feeling fine but Luke had the
horrible feeling that, for himself, the pain had only
just begun.

CHAPTER TWO

ANAHERA WASN'T LOOKING back at Luke and it felt like deliberate avoidance.

She had the nasal cannula hanging from her hands, one end attached to the oxygen cylinder, the other end ready to loop around their patient's ears, and she was looking at Sam.

'Keep really still for a tick, mate. I'm going to get a twelve-lead ECG printed out and then we'll see what's what.'

There were a few seconds' silence as the life pack captured a snapshot of the electrical activity of the heart and then printed out the graph. Luke looked around, as if he needed to remind himself of why he'd come here when he'd known about the risk. Okay, he'd thought that the worst he would face would be the memories but there'd always been the possibility that Ana might have come home again, hadn't there? He'd pushed it aside. He was only going to be on the island for a couple of days, in the company of his professional colleagues and a good friend. He wouldn't be facing anything he couldn't handle.

But here he was. Facing something he had no idea how to handle.

Anahera was *afraid* of him?

He'd hurt her *that* badly?

An unpleasant crawling sensation began to fill that space in his chest. He felt like a jerk. A complete bastard.

His gaze had tracked the other conference attendees standing in a sombre group waiting to hear the verdict on Charles Ainsley's chest pain but he ended up looking at Anahera again. This time her head was bent close to Sam's as they both studied the ECG. He could hear her voice.

'There's no sign of any ST segment elevation. I can't see any depression that might show myocardial ischaemia either, can you?'

She was speaking softly, her tone measured. He hadn't even remembered hearing her speak like this, maybe because the memory of the last time he had spoken to her had been so very different.

She'd been so angry that he'd finally tracked her down and called her while she'd been on shift at that hospital in Brisbane.

'What's the problem, Luke? Is London a bit boring? You feel like cheating on your wife again?'

She hadn't been about to let him say any of the things he'd wanted to say.

'I don't want to hear it. I never want to hear from you again. Ever...'

The anger had been contagious in the end. She'd hated him. How could love turn to hate as decisively as if a coin had been flipped?

It couldn't. That had been the conclusion Luke had come to. It couldn't happen if the love had been real. Yes, you could throw the coin in the air but there was magic in real love and the coin would always land the right side up.

He could never hate Anahera. Not in a million years. He would have given her the chance to explain. He would have listened.

And forgiven her anything.

Even now, he could forgive the way she was deliberately avoiding his gaze. How could he not when he'd seen that fear in her eyes?

'It's looking good, isn't it?' Charles was smiling. 'I told you it was only indigestion.'

'It's more likely it was angina, given how quickly it's gone with the GTN.'

'In any case, I'm fine.' Charles began to peel off the electrodes. 'I'm sorry to have given everyone a fright. It's my fault for forgetting my spray.'

'Keep this one,' Sam said. 'I'd still like to run some more tests. I've got a bench top assay for cardiac biomarkers. If I take a blood sample, I can pop into the laboratory here and have a result in no time.'

'Have a drink instead,' Charles said. 'And some of the amazing food.' He waved at his colleagues. 'Please carry on with your dinners,' he directed. 'Another life saved, here.'

A relieved buzz of conversation broke out and there were smiles all round. Anahera was still looking serious, however, as she coiled wires to tuck them into a pocket of the life-pack case.

He had to say something.

'It's good to see you, Ana. I...I wasn't expecting to.'

'No.' The wires had tangled a little and she shook them. 'I wasn't expecting to see you either.' Her soft huff of breath was an embryonic laugh. 'Silly, I guess. This is your field.' The wires were being coiled more tightly than necessary. 'It's a long way to come, though, and I wouldn't have thought you'd...'

What? She wouldn't have thought he'd want to come anywhere near this place again? The brief glance in his direction as her sentence trailed off made him feel like he was a stranger to her. Not someone to be afraid of now but someone to be ignored?

'I thought you were living in Brisbane.' Luke could have kicked himself the moment the words came out. It made it sound like the only reason he'd come back here was because he'd thought she was safely a very long way away.

But that was the truth, wasn't it?

'Sorry to disappoint you.' The pockets on the life pack were snapped shut, and Anahera got to her feet. 'I moved back home a couple of years ago.'

'I'm not disappointed.' He attempted a smile. 'And it *is* good to see you again.'

A lot of time had passed. Surely they could find a way to connect on some level? He wanted that, he realised. More than was probably good for him.

He wanted to see her eyes the way he remembered them, not full of fear that he might hurt her again. Or so distant he wasn't even being acknowledged for who he was. Or who he had been.

What he really wanted was to see Anahera smile, but it wasn't going to happen, was it?

And then it struck him. She wouldn't be afraid of him if she knew the truth. She wouldn't feel that avoiding him was the best way to cope either.

Something else crept into the odd mix of his feelings.

A glimmer of hope, perhaps?

Maybe this was an opportunity for both of them to lay some ghosts to rest. So that they could both move on with their lives without being haunted by what had happened between them.

'You stay.' Anahera zipped up the resus kit after Sam had taken the blood sample Charles had finally agreed was a good idea. 'You were coming here anyway. I can take all the gear back to the hospital.'

'Are you sure?' Sam was watching their patient re-join the gathering. 'I would quite like to keep an eye on him for a while. It's only going to take a few minutes to run the assay.'

'I'd like to see the laboratory again.' Much to Anahera's discomfort, Luke hadn't followed Charles to the other side of the meeting hall. 'It sounds like you've got more gear in there than there was when I was last here.'

'I'll bet. You should come and see the hospital, too. You wouldn't have had the CT scanner when you were here. Or the ventilator we've got for intensive care either.'

'You've got a CT scanner? Wow...'

'And Anahera, here, is a qualified intensive care nurse. She could pretty much do my job, to tell the truth. She did paramedic training in Brisbane, too. She's the best at intubating if you've got a difficult airway.' Sam laughed. 'But you probably know that. You guys must have kept in touch since you were here?'

'No.' Luke and Anahera spoke at the same time but their tones were very different. Luke's held regret. Anahera's was firm enough to sound like a reprimand. No wonder Sam gave her such a surprised glance.

She shrugged, her smile wry as she tried to excuse her tone. 'You know how many FIFOs we get. If we kept in touch with them all we'd never have time to do our jobs.'

Slipping the straps of the resus kit over her shoulders, Anahera bent to pick up the life pack in one hand and the oxygen cylinder in the other. She managed a brief glance at Luke. Another smile even, albeit a tight one. 'Enjoy your visit,' she said. 'I hope the conference is worthwhile.'

'Let me carry some of that for you.'

She avoided his gaze. 'I'm fine.'

Surely Luke could see that she needed to get away from him? Someone certainly could. Anahera could feel her mother's curious gaze all the way from where she was serving food again.

Had she been wrong in assuming that only she and Luke knew what had happened when he'd been on the island that first time? How close they had become?

If Vailea was busy putting two and two together, it could make things a whole heap more difficult.

'No, you're not.' Sam took the heavy life pack from her hand. 'Don't be such a heroine, Ana. You make us look bad.'

Sure enough, another man was coming towards them, clearly intent on helping.

Anahera smiled at Sam. 'Go on, then. Just to make you feel better.'

It would make her feel better, too, to have company as she walked away from Luke. She straightened her back. She had friends here. She used her now free hand to wave at her mother, who smiled back. She had family here, too. Luke was the outsider. If he presented a threat, she had plenty of people on her side.

And maybe he would retire gracefully. Sam had paused as Luke introduced him to the man who'd joined them.

'This is Harry. Sheikh Rahman al-Taraq. He's the person who's responsible for all of this. The man who's making it his mission to find a way to beat encephalitis, amongst other tropical nasties.'

A sheikh? Anahera blinked. This was all getting a little surreal.

Sam shook the sheikh's hand. 'I can't wait to talk to you,' he said. 'I've got a few minutes to spend in the laboratory and then I'll be back.'

'Mind if I come with you? I'd like to see how the labs are shaping up. We've put quite a lot of new equipment in there. Luke, you should come, too.'

'Oh?'

'I might have another job for you—after you've given your keynote address tomorrow. We've got a bit of research to set up, here. A clinical trial, I'm hoping.'

'I'm only here for a couple of days, Harry.' Luke's laugh sounded a bit forced. Nervous even?

If that was the case, he wasn't the only one feeling like that. Anahera started walking towards the golf cart again. This was getting rapidly worse. She needed a safe place to try and get her head around it all. She couldn't wait to get back to the hospital.

No…maybe she'd ask Hettie to stay on to start her night shift early. The safe place Anahera really needed was at home.

With her daughter.

* * *

Bessie, the housekeeper at the Lockhart mansion who looked after Hana when Anahera was at work, had been happy to babysit tonight.

'She's been no trouble,' she said. 'Went to bed and off to sleep like an angel.'

'That's where you need to go, too, Bessie. You look tired. Thank you so much for your help. I don't know what we'd do without you.'

The hug from the older woman was soft and squashy and full of love, and it took Anahera straight back to the kind of simplicity her childhood had been full of.

It made her want to cry.

'I am tired,' Bessie admitted. 'But I'm also very happy. Miss Caroline and Keanu are coming back very soon so I want the house to look perfect. We might have a wedding to get ready for.'

Anahera smiled. Keanu was another permanent doctor on Wildfire Island and, along with Sam, was a very good friend. Caroline was a Lockhart—the twin who had come into the world unscathed. 'It is very happy news. But don't go overdoing things.'

'Tell your mother that, too. She's working too hard. She has her job at the hospital and now she's taking on more work at that resort place.' Bessie shook her head as she gathered up her basket and cardigan. 'So much is happening on the island at the moment. I can't keep up…'

'I know. I feel like that, too.' Especially right now. 'But they're good things, Bessie. The mine closing has been a disaster for everybody, and Caroline's going to try and fix things. And the conference centre is going to create more jobs and bring in some money. I heard that there's going to be some new research projects happening, too. It's all good.'

But Bessie was frowning. 'You don't look so happy about it, Ana.'

Anahera summoned a genuine smile and words of reassurance as she waved Bessie off. She was going to have to be careful what showed on her face for the next few days. At least it would be a while before her mother came home. She had time to get things sorted in her head.

And her heart.

It was easy to do that. All she needed to do was tiptoe into the room where Hana lay sleeping in her small bed inside the mosquito netting that was printed with pretty pink butterflies. The nightlight was also a butterfly with glowing wings—because Hana had had a passion for butterflies ever since she'd been a baby—and it gave enough light to see her daughter's face clearly as Anahera pulled the netting back. She stroked the tangle of golden curls back from the little face and bent to press a gentle kiss to the soft olive skin of Hana's cheek.

Hana stirred. She didn't wake but she smiled in her sleep and her lips moved in a contented whisper.

'Mumma...'

'I'm here, darling. Sleep tight. Love you to the moon and back.'

She stole another kiss and then let the netting fall back to protect the precious little body, but for a long moment she didn't move. This was what she'd needed more than anything. To feel this love.

To remind herself that everything had been worth it and that she had no regrets.

There were things that she needed to do, like finding something for dinner, having a shower and finding a clean uniform for work tomorrow, but they could all wait until her mother was home. A quiet moment to herself seemed more important and Anahera chose to curl up on the old cane chair in the corner of the veranda that was bathed in moonlight and the scent of the nearby frangipani bushes.

Maybe it was the moonlight that was her undoing. Or the sweet scent of the tropical flowers. It was probably inevitable that she had to revisit her past, given the shock of seeing Luke, and maybe it was a necessary step in order to get past it and move forward again. Or at least get herself together enough to make sure her mother didn't guess the truth.

She couldn't know, could she? If she'd had even the tiniest suspicion she would never have made that casual remark that had sliced open old wounds for her own daughter.

'You had to rush away, though... Your wife was ill...'

It had been such a secret thing—their love affair.

How naïve had she been to think that had been because it had been so precious to them both? A private joy that might change when others knew about it?

But it had seemed like a natural progression, too, because of how it had started—as an almost telepathic conversation of glances and accidental touch as an undercurrent to the open conversations of two people getting to know each other. It had been Anahera who'd made the first move. Offering to show Luke the drama

of Sunset Beach had been an invitation to let whatever
had been happening between them grow and, for her,
that first kiss had only confirmed that her heart had
already been stolen.

And it would have changed things if others had
known. Her mother would have been afraid that she
would lose her. That Anahera would follow Luke back
to London and forget her island heritage. Her work
family would have worried about how they would re-
place her and she herself would have had to face the
possibility of giving up so much for a new life, and she
hadn't been ready for that. She had wanted to stay in
the safe bubble of no one else knowing for as long as
possible. To revel in the bright colours and extraordinary happiness of being so completely in love.

How ironic was it that she'd ended up having to
flee and start a new life anyway? Alone. Or so she'd
thought until the disruption and heartache had settled enough for her to realise what was happening to
her body.

And Luke? Well, he'd had his own reasons for
wanting to keep their love affair a secret and it hadn't
had anything to do with how precious it was, had it?

Tapping into that old anger wasn't going to help,
though. She'd made a conscious decision to let it go
the moment she'd first held Hana in her arms. To feel
thankful that it had happened even. Oh, it had resur-
faced sometimes in those first months of trying to
raise her daughter alone, when the fatigue and finan-
cial pressures and homesickness had got on top of her,
but coming back to Wildfire Island had fixed that.
She'd been back for more than two years now and she
had all the support she needed. A job that she loved

and the joy of watching her daughter grow up in the same place she had. A place filled with such extraordinary beauty and countless butterflies.

Her life was exactly the way she wanted it to be.

The last thing she'd expected—or wanted—was to be reminded that something was missing. The kind of something she'd found with Luke Wilson. The one thing she had known she would never find again, especially coming back to the isolation of her childhood home, but the sacrifice had been worth it.

For Hana.

Anahera was so happy here so there was a new anger to be found that her happiness had been ambushed like this. The sooner she could get Luke and all the associated baggage out of her head, the better.

She closed her eyes on a sigh, unable to ignore it any longer—the thing she knew wasn't going to be fixed when Luke left the island in a few days. Something that had always been there but which had suddenly become a whole lot bigger. Which might, in fact, get even worse when Luke had gone again.

The guilt that Luke had no idea he was Hana's father...

Something unexpected was happening for Luke, quite apart from seeing Anahera Kopu again.

A unique alchemy of personalities that was creating an energy that Luke had been unsuccessfully trying to resist ever since the 'meet and greet' cocktail party.

He recognised it as the kind of connection he'd found with Harry over the weeks he'd treated him in London. It was more than the beginnings of a significant friendship—it was a meeting of like minds that was inspirational enough to have the possibility of achieving something amazing.

Sam Taylor might appear to be extraordinarily laid back but there was a passion for what he did running quite close to the surface and his charm was a force to be reckoned with. Add that to the more brooding intelligence and determination of Harry, along with the kind of resources he had to make things happen, and Luke was finding himself to be the meat in an increasingly interesting sandwich.

Which was why—despite thinking it wasn't the best idea—he found himself visiting Wildfire Island's hospital during a break on the second day of the conference, when the other attendees had been taken out to one of the outer islands to go snorkelling and visit a turtle colony.

He didn't want it to seem like he was forcing his company on Anahera. If there was any chance of being able to talk and possibly resolve their unfinished business, it wasn't going to happen in front of other people. It wasn't going to happen as the result of a planned meeting either, but the hope of finding her by chance was fading after Luke's long walk along the beaches and through the village yesterday evening.

And this was a professional visit to the hospital. He and Sam had a lot to talk about.

The only space for that discussion appeared to be the room that staff gathered in to take a break. There was a kitchenette for preparing hot drinks or food and a small fridge that Sam opened to reveal an impressive stock of cold drinks. The couch looked as though it was a comfortable space to nap on a night shift, and Luke could see a neatly folded blanket and a couple of pillows tucked neatly behind it. A couple of reclining lounge chairs and a table filled the rest of the available space and one of the lounge chairs had an occupant.

'G'day, mate.'

'Jack—this is Luke Wilson. The encephalitis expert I was telling you all about. Luke—this is Jack Richards, our number-one helicopter pilot.'

Jack got to his feet and extended his hand. 'It's a privilege to meet you, Luke. You've certainly fired Sam up. Haven't seen him this excited in years.'

Luke shook his hand. 'It's an exciting development, that's for sure.'

'What would you like, Luke?' Sam still had the fridge door open. 'Something cold or a coffee or tea?'

'I'd love a cup of tea,' Luke admitted. 'Haven't had one since I left London and it's starting to feel a long time ago.'

'Might have one myself.' Sam grinned. 'Get in touch with my English roots.'

'Where are you from?'

'Up north. Did my training in Birmingham.'

'What brought you here?'

Sam shrugged. 'I love my sailing. Brought my yacht here to do a FIFO stint a few years back and I liked it so much I never left.'

There was more to the story than that, Luke thought, but he wasn't about to talk about it. He turned back to Jack, keen to ask what kind of challenges his job presented, but his gaze slid past the helicopter pilot as someone else entered the staffroom.

'Sam?' Anahera was holding a clipboard. 'Can I get you to sign off on the antibiotics for Kalifa Lui?' She stopped abruptly in the doorway as she spotted

Luke. He could see her neck muscles moving as she swallowed and then she cleared her throat as she broke the eye contact almost instantly. 'I think he's going to need some more Ventolin, too. The wheezing hasn't improved much since he came in.'

'Sure.' Sam paused in his task of making tea to take a pen from his shirt pocket and scribble on the clipboard. 'Have you persuaded him to stay overnight?'

'I'm working on it. I don't think he understands how serious a chest infection can be on top of his chronic lung disease, though. He wants to get back to work.'

'What work?' Jack asked. 'He's a miner and the mine's been closed. It's not safe any more.'

'They're not allowed down the mine but a lot of the men are working to try and improve the safety so they can open it again. They're desperate to get their livelihoods back.'

'I'll come and talk to him soon,' Sam said. 'And if I can't convince him, I'll get his wife, Nani, in here. She'll sort him out.'

'Okay…' Anahera turned to leave, and Luke stared at her. Was she not even going to acknowledge him?

'Stay for a few minutes,' Sam said. 'There's something Luke and I are going to discuss and it involves you.'

'I…I need to get back to Kalifa.'

'He's had his first dose of antibiotics, hasn't he?'

'Yes.'

'And his first nebuliser is still going?'

'Yes.'

'And one of the aides is in the ward with him who

can come and find us if there's any deterioration in his condition?'

Anahera just nodded this time. Still without looking at Luke, she came and sat down on one of the kitchen chairs around the table.

Sam put down two mugs of tea and gestured to Luke to take another seat. Jack watched them.

'Maybe I'll leave you to it. Go and polish the red bird or something.'

'You're welcome to stay,' Sam said. 'In fact, you'll probably be involved as much as Ana. Have a seat.'

Jack looked intrigued. Anahera was looking wary.

'What's going on?' she asked.

'You both know the really exciting news.'

'You talked about it enough yesterday.' Jack grinned. 'We have a vaccination available for M'Langi encephalitis that's been approved for clinical trials.'

'That's right.'

Jack's grin faded as he looked at Luke. 'From what Sam was saying, it was one hell of an opening address that your friend made.' He turned to Anahera. 'You had a day off yesterday so you weren't here to hear that story, were you? About the sheikh and his investment?'

'Ah…no. I did briefly see the sheikh at the conference centre and I also heard about the new vaccination. The whole island's talking about it.' She smiled at Luke. 'It's amazing news.'

'It's thanks to Luke that it's happened,' Sam said. 'There's already the vaccination for Japanese encephalitis but there were plenty of other varieties to choose to work on next. It was Luke's connection to these islands that made M'Langi the lucky one.'

'I've never forgotten my time here,' Luke said quietly. 'I think about it every day.'

A flush of colour darkened Anahera's olive skin. The hidden message had been received loud and clear. It hadn't been just the island that he'd thought about every day, had it? He'd been thinking about *her*...

'But the thanks should go to Harry,' he continued. 'He's the one who's put an extraordinary amount of time and money into getting this vaccination developed.'

'Which he couldn't have done if you hadn't saved his life.' Sam turned his gaze to Anahera. 'You should have heard him talking,' he told her. 'There wasn't a dry eye in the house by the time he'd finished telling us how close to death he was when he got encephalitis. How Luke was there with him twenty-four seven in the ICU, fighting for his life as if it was his own. That it was that kind of devotion that made Harry determined to give something back to thank him and to try and stop other people having to go through what he went through.'

The praise had been embarrassing yesterday. He'd only been doing his job after all, but watching Anahera's reaction to the story made it feel very different. There was something in her eyes that was making him feel proud instead of embarrassed. There was respect there. And something warmer—as if she was feeling proud of him, too?

'I always knew you'd go on to do great things,' she said softly. 'It's a great story.'

'Sounds like you have, too. Paramedic and ICU qualifications? An expert in difficult airway management? How long did you stay in Brisbane?'

'About two years.' Anahera's glance flicked away the moment Brisbane was mentioned, and Luke could almost feel a change in temperature around him as any perceived warmth got sucked out.

She really didn't want to talk to him about Brisbane, did she?

Why? Had the opportunity for postgraduate training been compelling for more than professional reasons? Because it had meant a fresh start—away from the place she had met him?

No. He was reading too much into it. She hadn't cared that much or she wouldn't have dismissed him with such devastating effect after all the effort he'd made to track her down. She'd moved on with her life, that was all. And what she'd done with it was none of his business.

Fine. He could move on, too. He could start with this conversation.

'Harry has plans for some research projects that can only happen here,' he said. 'One of them involves travel to some of the outer islands, which is where you come in, Jack. He's only just heard about this M'Langi tea and he thinks it could be important.'

'Why?' Anahera was frowning. 'It only has insect repellent qualities, doesn't it?'

'Exactly,' Sam said with satisfaction. 'Controlling the mosquito population by reducing habitats that support breeding and personal protection by clothing and repellents are the mainstay of prevention of mosquito-borne disease. Repellents are only ever applied externally. It could be a real breakthrough to discover something effective that can be taken systemically. Did you know that there were an estimated seventy-seven thousand deaths worldwide in 2013 from encephalitis?'

'You've got some data on which islands have the lowest incidence of encephalitis, haven't you?' Luke asked. 'That's where we'll need to go to collect samples and find out exactly how they brew that tea.'

Sam nodded. 'From memory, I'm pretty sure it's French Island, and that's where the particular hibiscus bushes that they make the tea from grow, but I'll check.'

'French Island?'

'Apparently there was a shipwreck there long ago. A French square-rigged sailing vessel. The crew survived and so we have a fair bit of French blood mingling with the islanders'. We still get some French sailors turning up, intrigued by the historic link.'

Curiously, Anahera didn't seem to want to be hearing any of this. She got to her feet.

'I really need to get back to my patients. I can't see how any of this involves me.'

'You're due to do the clinic on French Island in the next couple of days, aren't you?'

'Oh…you want me to collect some tea-leaves? Talk to the locals?'

'No. I want you to take Luke with you.'

That shocked her enough to freeze her movements, except for the direction of her gaze, which flew to Luke in alarm. 'But the conference finishes today, doesn't it? Don't you have to get back to London?'

There was that fear again. It was just a bit over the top, wasn't it? He'd been keeping his distance and it had to be obvious he wasn't going to force his company—or anything else—on her.

'Harry's persuaded me to stay on for a bit. To set up the research projects and get the protocols in place for a clinical trial of the vaccination.'

Anahera turned to Sam. 'Maybe you should do the clinic instead of me, then. I don't have anything to do with research and you love it.'

She was trying to avoid him again. Luke could feel himself frowning and barely registered Sam's smile as he spoke.

'Don't worry, we'll sort out the logistics. Why don't I give you a tour of the hospital while we talk? You'll be wanting to get back for the last session of the conference.'

Jack got to his feet as well. 'Time I did some work, too. Nice to meet you, Luke. I look forward to transporting you around the islands very soon.'

Anahera was leading the way as they all left the staffroom. The layout of the hospital still felt familiar to Luke. The U-shaped building with small wards on one side, Outpatients, kitchens and the staffroom in the middle and the ED, ICU and Radiography— that now, apparently, had gone high-tech with CT and ultrasound equipment available—on the other side. The wide covered walkway linking the wings surrounded a lush tropical garden that boasted a pretty pond in its centre.

The walkway was as spacious as he remembered and the overhead fans kept everything deliciously cool as they added to a sea breeze coming in from the garden.

There was more than a breeze coming in from the garden at the moment, though. An older woman who was carrying a small child could be seen ahead of them.

And, again, Anahera froze.

'*Bessie*…what are you doing here? What's happened?'

Luke could see that the child—a tiny girl—had been crying. Her hand was wrapped in what looked like a bloodstained tea towel.

'It's nothing to worry about,' the woman said. 'Just a little cut but it took a while to stop the bleeding and Hana got upset. I said we'd come and find Dr Sam and Mummy.'

Mummy? One of the other nurses here, perhaps? Luke, like everyone else, had stopped walking. Now the island woman stopped, too, as the child in her arms wriggled free. As soon as the girl's feet touched the floor, she was running. The tea towel unwound itself and fell to the floor as she threw her arms up in the air.

'Mumma…' The word was a sob.

Anahera was crouching, arms out, ready to catch the little girl. She scooped her up and held her close, pressing her cheek to a fluffy cloud of pale curls as she murmured reassurance.

And then she looked up and her gaze met Luke's.

He knew he must look like an idiot, with his jaw still hanging open, but this was the biggest shock yet since he'd set foot on Wildfire Island again.

There could be no mistaking the relationship between these two with the way this child had her arms wound so tightly around Anahera's neck and the palpable comfort she was clearly receiving from having found the person she needed most.

Anahera was a *mother*?

He had to swallow his shock. At least no one else seemed to have noticed. Jack was behind him and Sam was focussed on the child.

'Have you got a sore finger, sweetheart? Can you show Dr Sam?'

'It's all right, darling,' Anahera said. 'It's not going to hurt. We just want to see.'

A tiny hand appeared from behind her mother's neck and then a forefinger uncurled itself. The cut was quite deep but small.

'She found a piece of broken glass,' Bessie said unhappily. 'She was helping me clean out a cupboard.'

'You know what?' Sam asked cheerfully.

The small head moved slowly from side to side.

'I think I've got a plaster that's just the right size for a finger like that. And it's got a picture on it. Do you know what that picture might be?'

Big dark eyes widened. 'A flutterby?'

Sam grinned. 'Sorry, not a butterfly this time, button. Would a princess do instead? A Cinderella plaster?'

The smile was tentative.

'Didn't Cinderella have butterflies on her dress?' Anahera said. 'I'm sure she did. We've got the book at home, haven't we, Hana?'

Hana. So this exquisite child had a name that sounded like an echo of her mother's shortened name. She had her mother's gorgeous dark eyes, too, but her skin was much lighter and her hair very different from Anahera's midnight black.

'She's beautiful,' Luke heard himself saying aloud. 'How old is she?'

The moment the words left his mouth he realised, with what felt like a body blow, that it was possible he was looking at his own daughter here.

For a long moment there was a silence so complete it felt like everyone else here knew the significance of what the answer to his query could be. In the end, it was Hana who spoke.

'I'm *free*,' she told him.

'Three,' Anahera corrected her. 'Three and a *half*, even.'

The mental calculations were so easy to make, it took only a few seconds. Add on nine months for a pregnancy. Count up the years and months since he and Anahera had had that last, incredible night on Sunset Beach.

The difference was six months. There was no way that Hana was his child.

It should have been a huge relief.

So why was he left feeling so crushed?

Maybe because it was the final proof that Anahera hadn't cared enough. She'd moved on so fast she'd found someone else and become pregnant in the short space of a few months. For all Luke knew, Hana's father was also here on Wildfire Island. He might come through the same door any moment now.

Luke swallowed hard as he checked his watch. 'I might head back, Sam,' he said. 'We'll have plenty of time for this tour in the next few days, and, as you reminded me, I don't want to miss the last session of the conference.'

He didn't look back as he fired his parting words. 'It's what I actually came here for, after all.'

CHAPTER THREE

'WHAT'S UP, ANA?'

'Nothing.' Anahera didn't look up from her task of packing the large plastic bin that was on the bench, surrounded by a wide array of supplies.

'You don't seem yourself, that's all.' Sam was leaning against the doorframe of this storage room in the hospital's theatre annexe, having delivered the chilli bin with the lunch that Vailea had packed for the team doing the clinic run to French Island today.

Anahera turned away from him to stare at a shelf. 'Don't tell me we're out of urine dipsticks…I know we've got people who aren't managing their type two diabetes very well on French Island.'

Sam took a step into the room, reached past her shoulder and picked up the jar that had been right in front of her.

'Thanks.' Anahera cringed inwardly. 'Guess I was having a "man" look.'

'If you're worried about blood-glucose levels, a blood test is far more sensitive.'

'I know that.' The words came out as an unintentional snap and she hurriedly modified her tone. 'If the level's high enough to show up in urine then we'll know treatment is urgent. I've found that the occasional patient is more likely to agree to give a sample of urine than get stuck with a needle, even if it is just in a finger. I've already packed the BGL kit. I need the dipsticks for the antenatal checks, too.'

'Okay…'

She could feel Sam watching her. Maybe she hadn't undone the damage that that uncharacteristic snap had done.

'Sorry,' she muttered. 'I didn't sleep that well last night and I guess I'm a bit put out, having to take someone else with us today. It'll put us under pressure to get through the clinic cases so I have time to take him into the village to talk to people and get samples of the leaves or bark or whatever it is they use off the hibiscus plants.'

'Hmm…' Sam still hadn't left the room. 'Why is it that I get the impression you don't like Luke? I'm going to be working with the guy and he seems great. Is there something about him I should know?'

'No.'

'But you've met him before. You know him better than I do.'

Anahera almost laughed at the understatement. She could only hope that her smile wasn't wry.

'He's an awesome doctor. Hard-working and very, very smart. And he cares a lot about his patients.' She was keeping her hands busy, packing syringes and swabs into the plastic bin. Then she reached for the pregnancy test kits and had to close her eyes for a heartbeat. Sam was a good friend. Maybe he deserved to know that Luke wasn't completely honest. That he couldn't be trusted.

'I know…you should have heard that sheikh guy talking about him. Harry made him sound like God's gift to medicine.'

'Mmm…' It really was time to change the subject. 'Has Jack called to say the chopper's ready yet? We should get going soon. And if Luke's not here on time, we'll have to go without him.

'I'll find out.'

It was a relief to be left alone to finish her packing. Anahera really needed a few minutes to herself. A few deep breaths should do it, along with bringing her focus back to the task at hand so that she didn't find herself staring at something on a shelf that she couldn't see.

But the deep breathing didn't do what it was supposed to do. It didn't even melt the edges off that hard knot that seemed to be lodged in her belly.

Guilt, that was what it was.

She'd told Sam she hadn't slept that well last night but the truth was she'd tossed and turned so much that she'd barely slept at all.

It didn't matter how many times she went over and over that incident at the hospital when Hana had been brought in because she couldn't change the impressions she'd been left with. If anything, they only became crisper.

For a start, there'd been that unexpected and shocking reaction to seeing them together. A flash of imagining what it could have been like if they had become a family. A slicing pain of loss so deep that it was fortunate it had vanished as instantly as it had attacked.

Luke's face had been as easy to read as a large-print book. She'd seen the shock of discovering that she was a mother. Had seen the moment when it had occurred to him that *he* could possibly be Hana's father. And then she'd seen something that was shocking to *her*. *Disappointment?*

Did he want a child?

Even if he didn't, he had the right to know he had one, didn't he?

Oh, God…the guilt stone was getting steadily bigger and it had sharp edges that were giving her shafts of pain like colic.

Maybe reasoning would soften the edges, seeing that deep breathing hadn't done the trick.

She was deceiving him for everybody's sake.

His, Hana's, her mother's and her own.

She'd been over this ground so many times it was a familiar route. It was ironic how that casual conversation Luke had had with Sam yesterday was always her starting point.

Because one of those French sailors, intrigued by the history of the island, had been her father.

He'd come here, fallen in love with both the islands and her mother, and they had married and built a house on Atangi—the main island of this group. Her father, Stefan, had planned to create a premium tourist destination where people could come and sail and dive. It would bring money in to the islands and allow him to do what he loved most for the rest of his life.

He'd missed his homeland, though, and he'd taken Vailea and baby Anahera back to France for an extended visit to meet his family. They'd lived on the outskirts of Paris for three months.

'It was *so* cold,' her mother always said. 'And I couldn't speak the language. Even with you and Stefan there, it was the loneliest time. I wanted to be with him but part of me was slowly dying.'

They'd come back to the islands but things had changed. The islands were a place for a holiday for Stefan now and they couldn't be real life. Heartbroken, her parents had finally agreed they had to live apart. Vailea would visit Paris once a year in summer and Stefan would come to Atangi during the French winters. He'd never made it, even once, however, because he'd died after a diving mishap that had given him a fatal dose of the bends.

The first-hand knowledge of the heartbreak that trying to live in different worlds could produce was a sound starting point, wasn't it? Anahera had lived in Brisbane where the climate was far more like her homeland than London could ever be, but she'd ended up miserable and homesick. When she thought of London, it was always grey and people had to wear thick clothing and carry umbrellas all the time. Had she really thought—in those heady weeks of being so utterly in love—that she could have gone to live in London with Luke?

It could never have worked.

Hana would have to go there, though, if he knew he was her father. He would, quite rightfully, expect to be able to spend extended time with his daughter and, with his career, it wasn't likely that he could take time off to visit a remote part of the Pacific at regular intervals.

It was too easy to imagine the worst-case scenario. Arguments about schooling that might lead to a battle not to have Hana sent to an English boarding school. A taste of a different life that might lead to her teenage daughter deciding she would rather live full time with her father in a place that offered so much more in terms of social life and excitement.

Maybe it was the fear of loss that was the real driving force in this deception.

And, if she was completely honest, Anahera didn't want to share her precious daughter with the man who had broken her heart. He didn't deserve to have the unconditional love that this amazing little girl with the biggest heart in the world gave so freely.

Did that make her a bad person?

If it did, Anahera had decided long ago that she would live with the guilt of being one.

How much easier had that burden been to carry when Luke had been just a memory? Having him here in person was so much worse.

Unbearable even.

And now she had to spend a whole day in his company?

She had to press a hand to her belly as another knife-like cramp took hold.

'Ana?' Sam's voice floated through the doorway. 'Jack's all set and Luke's already at the helipad.' He came through the door just as Anahera straightened her back and summoned all her willpower to ignore the pain. 'Let me carry that bin for you.'

Getting a bird's-eye view of the islands from the cockpit of a helicopter was so much more spectacular than the limited scope of a small plane's window.

Luke was sitting in the front beside Jack and he had a grin on his face. 'Look at that...the sea's so clear you can just about see the coral in the reef. And the fish...'

'Gorgeous, isn't it? I never get sick of my office.' Jack's voice came through the headphones Luke was wearing. 'That's Atangi, there. The biggest island by land mass and the one that's been settled the longest. That's where the main schools are. It's where you grew up, isn't it, Ana?'

'Yes.' Anahera was sitting in the cabin of the helicopter, behind Luke so he couldn't see her. 'Until Mum started working at the hospital. We moved to the village on Wildfire after that and I took the boat to school.'

Luke hadn't known that. What had they talked about all those years ago? Maybe he'd done too much talking and not enough listening but it was too late to start now. Anahera had barely glanced at him when she'd arrived at the helipad and he hadn't been able to think of anything to say after a simple 'Good morning' because there'd been too many questions zipping through his head, starting with who looked after her daughter when she was at work and what did her husband do? And then he'd taken notice of her hands as she'd helped Jack load supplies into the chopper and he'd seen the absence of a wedding ring and that only led to more questions that he'd probably never get the chance to ask because it seemed like Anahera didn't even want to talk to him.

He shouldn't have let Harry and Sam talk him into extending his visit but that had been before he'd known about Anahera's daughter. When he'd still had that vague hope that maybe he and Anahera could clear the air between them. That he would be able to finally explain...

The chance of that happening had evaporated in the

shock of finding out how conclusively Anahera had already moved on with her life. Why would he want to make things harder for himself by reopening old scars?

But what if she wasn't married? If whoever she had moved on with was no longer in her life?

No. He didn't want to go there. Didn't even want to think about it.

'What's that island?' he asked to distract himself. 'That round one, off to the left there. I never visited the other islands when I was here last time. I had no idea there were so many.'

'There are a lot. Most of them are uninhabited, though. That round one is Opuru. It got evacuated after a tsunami a decade or two ago and that's when the village on Wildfire got built. Before that, it was only the Lockharts and their house staff that lived here. The mine workers would all commute, mostly from Atangi.'

'Where's French Island?'

'A bit farther out. Not as big as Atangi and not as mountainous as Wildfire. It's got a lovely reef, though, and there's still the wreck of the ship it was named for. Divers love it. With the sea so clear, there's a point on one of the hills where you can see the bones of the whole ship. It's pretty spectacular.'

'I'd love to see that.'

'I could show you,' Jack said. 'We might have time, depending on how many people turn up for the clinic, of course. I stay close, in case Ana needs a hand.'

'I'd like to help with the clinic, too. If that's okay, Ana.'

'It won't be necessary.' Anahera's voice was cool. 'A lot of the people on this island don't speak much

English so I'd have to translate everything and that would just slow us down. Jack and I do this on a regular basis and we've never had a problem we couldn't deal with. But thanks for the offer.'

Luke lapsed into silence as the helicopter dipped lower, heading for the landing point on French Island. The warning was clear and it was timely. If it felt like this to get a professional offer rejected, he would be wise not to make himself vulnerable on a personal level.

He wasn't wanted. Maybe he never really had been.

The patients waiting for the clinic to open were already sheltering from the sun under the spreading branches of an enormous fig tree.

Anahera could see a couple of pregnant women, mothers holding small children and a few elderly people who had family members there to support them. As she greeted everybody on the way in to open up the clinic building, she was already making a mental note of everything she would need to do. Rough bandages on limbs meant a wound that would need cleaning and dressing, possibly suturing. Her diabetic patients needed testing to make sure their blood-sugar levels were under control, either by medication or the lifestyle changes she was trying to encourage. The people with hypertension needed their blood pressure checked and, if the levels weren't improving, she'd need to talk to them about how compliant they were being with taking their tablets.

Antenatal checks for the pregnant women were important, too, and sometimes it took a lot of persuasion to get the mothers-to-be to leave their families in order to go to the mainland to give birth. Lani was worrying her at the moment.

'Your baby is still upside down,' Anahera told Lani when it was her turn for a consultation. 'I'd like you see the obstetrician when she comes to Wildfire next week. Can you come across on the boat? Like you did for the ultrasound?'

Lani's gaze shifted to the silent, elderly woman who was sitting on a chair beside the window, and she lowered her voice. 'There's no one else to care for my mother during the day. My father is out fishing and my husband works on Atangi. It's difficult… especially since my brother and his family went to live in Australia.'

'I know.' Lani's mother had had a stroke a year ago and had been left with a disability that needed constant care. She had lost the use of one arm, her speech was unintelligible to anyone other than Lani and she had difficulty swallowing.

'Leave it with me, Lani. I'll arrange something. Maybe we can get someone to come here to help. Or we can arrange for your mother to come with you, like she has today.'

What would happen if the flying obstetrician deemed the birth high risk and advised Lani to go to Australia for the last weeks of her pregnancy was another problem. Anahera would need to bring it up with Sam and the other staff at their next clinical meeting. They might have to admit Lani's mother to the hospital to care for her until Lani was home again.

The morning flew by as Anahera treated her patients. Whenever she went outside to call the next person in, it was impossible not to look around to see how Luke was passing the time.

She'd been very unwelcoming, telling him his help wasn't necessary. She could imagine the look that Sam would give her if he found out. Or what he would say.

You had a doctor there and you made him just sit and wait for you? That's crazy, Ana. We need all the help we can get here. You know that.

She did know that. So the new guilt, added to what was already there, was taking the shine off a day that she normally loved. But she remembered how well they had worked together all those years ago. How they'd felt like the perfect partnership right from the first case they'd shared, and she didn't want to feel that professional rapport again. Things were hard enough as they were.

And Luke didn't seem to be feeling bad about being left out. When she went outside with Lani and looked at the long bench under the fig tree, he was no longer sitting there. In fact, half of the waiting patients weren't there any more either. A burst of laughter and a child's gleeful shriek revealed what was going on. A game of barefoot football. Village children had gathered and it seemed like the captains of the two teams were Jack and Luke.

For a moment Anahera watched the game, a smile spreading over her face, and, for the first time today, the knot in her stomach eased a little.

Luke looked so happy. He didn't need to speak an island dialect to connect to these children and they were loving this game. Could they tell that the way he was trying to block their access to the improvised goal was all for show and he was actually making it easier for them? The triumphant shouting when Luke was dramatically waving his fists in the air to indicate frustrated defeat suggested that they didn't and the joyful laughter meant that it didn't matter even if they did know.

And then a small boy tripped as he was running and fell hard, raising a cloud of dust from the bare patch of ground. Luke was there before the dust even began to settle, scooping the child up and settling him on one hip as he checked for any injury.

Anahera could see the concern on his face. The gentle way he was examining small limbs. And then he tickled the little boy and they both burst into laughter.

The stone in Anahera's belly seemed to turn into jelly.

She had forgotten how great Luke had been with children. That instant rapport that paved the way for making it easy for him to care for them. That patience and kindness that always won over even the most frightened children in the end.

It had been one of the first things she had loved about him.

She had thought about what a wonderful father he would make one day and how his children would adore him.

It wasn't the heat or dust that was making her throat close up.

It felt more like overwhelming sadness.

Luke set the child down on his feet and he ran off to join his friends. Luke was still grinning and he wiped dusty hands on his already smeared white shirt and then he looked around and caught sight of Anahera and the grin faded. He looked wary rather than happy now.

As if his change in mood was contagious, the game broke up. Anahera had to blink back tears. The happiness had been snuffed out and it felt like it was her fault.

'Alika? Can you come inside now, please? It's your turn...'

Finally, the clinic was over.

Luke watched as Anahera locked the door of the simple hut. Jack picked up the supply bin, which was almost empty, in one hand. He had the chilli bin that had held the sandwiches and cold drinks they'd had for lunch in the other.

'I'm going to drop these back to the chopper and then have a swim,' he said. 'Luke's already had a dip but I'm still filthy from that game of footy. Take your time in the village, Ana, but it'd be nice to get back to Wildfire before dark.'

'I thought you were going to come with us. Didn't you want to show Luke the shipwreck?'

'You know where it is.' Jack began to walk away. 'Have fun.'

Luke eyed Anahera. She met his gaze but neither of them smiled.

'Let's go, then,' he said. 'I've got all the snap-lock bags I need for samples and a notebook for recording information about the tea brewing.'

'Okay.' Anahera's nod was brisk. 'It's not too far to the village but we'd need to take a slightly longer route if you want to see the shipwreck.'

Did he want more time with Anahera?

This was an unexpected opportunity as he'd also thought that Jack would be joining them for the visit to the village. And it could well be the only chance he was going to get to have a private conversation with her.

'Yes.' His hesitation had been brief. 'I would like that. Very much.'

Their path took them uphill along a forest track, and Luke wasn't bothered by the silence between them because it added to the magic of the rainforest. It had been so long since he'd walked a track like this and he'd forgotten how intricately intertwined the plant life was. Spaces between the tall, smooth trunks of the trees that stretched to form the canopy were crowded with tree ferns and palms and ginger plants. There were dense tangles of vines that were a startling contrast to spectacular bursts of colour from orchids. Overhead branches had epiphytes and aerial moss competing for room. The raucous screech of parrots and a hum of insects were the only sounds other than twigs breaking beneath their feet.

They emerged from the forest into an area that had been cleared enough for grass to grow. There were some goats farther up the hill but Anahera led him towards a rocky patch that looked disconcertingly close to where the ground fell away steeply.

'Don't go too close to the edge,' she said. 'And test the rocks before you stand or sit on any of them. Sometimes one goes rolling off. The big ones are safe.' She scrambled carefully over some small rocks to climb onto the biggest one that jutted out towards the sea. Luke followed and found there was plenty of room for two people and the surface was quite flat. It provided a viewing platform with a stunning panorama of the ocean a long way below. The water was an astonishing shade of turquoise and so clear the ghostly outline of the ancient shipwreck was instantly recognisable.

'Wow…' Luke shaded his eyes from a sun that was getting lower in the sky and stared down. 'That's amazing…'

'Mmm. I love it here.' To Luke's consternation, Anahera walked calmly to the edge of the rock and folded herself gracefully to sit down with her legs dangling in space.

He followed a little more cautiously.

And there they were. Totally alone with the most stunning view imaginable spread out in front of them, with countless islands in every direction and the curve of reefs sheltering some of them and the changes in sea colour from pale turquoise to the almost navy blue of the deepest ocean. The intense heat of the day had faded and a gentle breeze was playing with the long strands of Anahera's ponytail. As if to make the moment perfect, a gorgeous gold-and-black butterfly came within touching distance as it flew past.

Luke was unlikely to get a better opening to a conversation.

'How cool is that?' He smiled. 'A flutterby.'

A huff of laughter escaped Anahera and it was the first time Luke had seen a genuine smile on her face in his presence. The kind that made the corners of her eyes crinkle and her whole face light up.

'You're not three, Luke. I don't think you get to call them a flutterby.'

'But why not?' It was so good to see her smile. It felt like that impenetrable barrier had just become transparent. 'It's such a brilliant word. It's exactly what they do, isn't it? Look...'

Sure enough, the stunning insect was fluttering, rising and then swooping as if it needed to explore its surroundings thoroughly.

'It's a beauty,' Anahera murmured. 'Hana would love it. She's had this thing for butterflies since she was tiny. I had her outside having a kick in the sun when she was only a few weeks old and she saw her first butterfly. That was when she smiled for the first time and it was the biggest grin.' Remembering it was making Anahera smile again and her expression was so tender it made Luke's heart ache.

'She's a very beautiful little girl. You must be very proud of her.'

'I am.'

'And her dad? He must be over the moon to have a daughter like Hana.'

There was a moment's silence that felt heavy. Awkward.

'He's not in the picture,' Anahera said.

Oh... Luke's heart missed a beat. 'Did...you meet him in Australia? At the hospital?' Had he been another doctor, like himself, perhaps? Or maybe a paramedic when Anahera was doing that part of her postgraduate training?

She seemed to be still watching the path the butterfly had taken, even though it had disappeared. 'He was a doctor.' She took a long inward breath that came out as a sigh. 'I had Hana in Brisbane and...and there was never any chance of a relationship with her father so...so I came home. To my family. My mother raised me by herself. History repeats itself sometimes, doesn't it?'

It didn't have to. The flash of bitterness that Anahera had chosen a path that didn't include him was ugly enough for Luke to squash it instantly, before its poison could tarnish this moment. He cleared his throat and searched for a way to change the conversation's trajectory.

'She looks very happy. When she doesn't have a sore finger.'

'She is. She loves the islands.' Anahera's tone lightened. 'There are more butterflies here.'

It was a neat, verbal circle that indicated that that topic of conversation was over. The silence was longer this time but it didn't feel so awkward. If anything, Luke was feeling more hopeful. Knowing that Anahera wasn't in a committed relationship with Hana's father made it more acceptable, somehow, to revisit the past.

'I'd forgotten,' Luke said quietly, 'how beautiful so many things are here. Like the ocean and the forest and the wildlife. The only thing I never forgot... was you.'

He could feel the way Anahera froze beside him. Could feel the transparency of that barrier fading so that it was becoming solid again. And then she moved, pulling her legs up over the edge of the rock and getting to her feet in one fluid movement.

Her voice was like ice. 'Did you tell your wife, Luke? About cheating on her?'

'No.' His response was so quiet he didn't think she'd heard.

'Maybe you should.'

'I can't do that.' Luke got to his feet slowly. His muscles felt heavy. Stiff. 'My wife died, Ana. Years ago. A few weeks after I left Wildfire.'

She was shocked. Her face turned back towards him. Her mouth opened and then closed, as if there'd been no words available. The breeze was still playing with the long strands of her ponytail and a few hairs caught on her lips but she didn't brush them away, she just kept staring at Luke.

'She was sick.' The words sounded wooden. The movement of her hand as she finally scraped the hair free of her lips was impatient. 'I knew that was why you had to rush back.'

'Not exactly. She woke up.'

The stare was back again, this time accompanied by a grimace of incomprehension. Disbelief, perhaps.

Luke's mouth felt dry. This wasn't exactly the scene he'd imagined when he'd hoped for the chance to tell Anahera the truth. Sitting on Sunset Beach, holding hands might have been nearer the mark. Standing on a windswept rock with a dangerous cliff and the skeleton of a long-ago wrecked ship far below made it all far too dramatic.

'She'd been in a coma for three years,' he said. 'It was the first time I'd been away from her and she'd opened her eyes and asked where I was. Yes, I had to rush back.'

Again, Anahera had no words.

'And, yes,' Luke continued quietly. 'I was married when I was with you but it didn't feel like cheating. My marriage was over the day of the accident that put Jane into that coma, although it took a very long time for me to accept that.'

'Was…was she still awake when you got back to London?'

'No. She never opened her eyes again. I sat with her every day and held her hand but she just slipped away, bit by bit. And then it was finally over. After the funeral, I tried to call you. Someone at the hospital told me you'd gone to Brisbane so I kept trying. I wanted you to know…but…'

He didn't need to finish his sentence. He could see that Anahera remembered that conversation as well as he did. And now she knew she'd accused him and judged him guilty without knowing all the facts. She looked…appalled. Her gaze slid away from his and, after a long silence, she cleared her throat.

'We should get to the village,' she said. 'If we don't go now, we won't have enough time before Jack wants to leave.'

They walked in silence again, but Luke was okay with that. Anahera needed time to process what he'd told her. Maybe it would make a difference or maybe it wouldn't, but that was okay, too. He'd been able to tell her the truth and that was enough to bring a sense of peace.

It was Anahera who broke the silence, when they'd left the forest track and were walking under an avenue of coconut palms near the beach.

'How did it happen?' she asked. 'The accident, I mean?'

'Jane was a competitive swimmer. She used to train at a local pool early every morning as soon as it opened. Sometimes the only other person there was the guy who ran the aquatic centre. On that morning, he'd been doing something in the office and when he came out he saw her floating face down in the pool. They think she must have slipped on the tiles and hit her head. He got her out and started CPR but…it was too late. She'd been without oxygen for too long.'

'That must have been devastating. I'm…I'm so sorry, Luke.'

Was she sorry for what he'd been through or did the apology include the way she'd treated him?

The look in her eyes suggested it was both. Maybe she wanted to say something more but their arrival at the village had been spotted and a bunch of children were running towards them.

'Football, mister! Come with us…' The small boy who'd taken the tumble in the game they'd had earlier took hold of Luke's hand and tugged on it. Small, grinning faces surrounded them.

Anahera shook her head and spoke to the children in their own language. The persuasive sounds turned to disappointed ones but the small boy still kept hold of his hand as they walked between the first bures of the village.

'Marama, the woman we're coming to see, lives here.' Anahera pointed out one of the simple dwellings. 'She's going to show you how she makes the tea and take us to where the bushes grow.'

Except Marama wasn't at home. Anahera asked the children but they shrugged and shook their heads so they wandered farther into the village. Luke recognised a young pregnant woman he'd seen attending the clinic today. She had one arm around the older woman who'd been with her, supporting her shuffling gait, and she had a basket in her other hand, filled with what looked like taro roots.

'Marama's in Tane's house,' she told Anahera in response to her query. 'He's her son and he's very sick.'

Even if they hadn't been looking for Marama they would have had to go and see what was wrong.

And something was very wrong.

Tane—a young man in his early twenties—was in the grip of a seizure as Anahera and Luke entered the bure. Several people were crouched around him, trying to hold his limbs still. A woman was trying to put a stick between his teeth.

Anahera touched the woman's wrist and spoke quietly but urgently. The woman took the stick away and one by one the others let go of the man's body. Someone shifted a cooking pot farther away and another ran outside.

'I've told him to go and get Jack,' Anahera told Luke. 'We need the resus kit. And a stretcher.'

'Can you find out what's going on? Do you know this man? Is he epileptic?'

'Not that I know of. He's running a high temperature. I can feel the heat from here.' She began asking questions of the people around her and then she translated the answers.

'His wife, Kura, says that Tane was complaining of a bad headache yesterday and he was shivering. Marama gave him herbal tea but it didn't help. He was very sleepy this morning, which was why they didn't bring him up to the clinic. This is the first seizure he's had.'

'No history of any recent head injury?'

'No.'

'I can't tell if there's any rash.' Luke leaned closer

to peer at Tane's bare chest but the dark skin was gleaming with sweat.

'The light's not good enough. Here...I've got a penlight torch.'

'Great. I'd like to check his pupils as soon as I can. Might give us a clue to his intracranial pressures.'

The jerking of the man's limbs was lessening. His eyelids flickered and he began groaning and then his eyes opened and he started shouting—a look of absolute terror on his face. Luke wasn't going to get a chance to check pupil sizes and reaction to light any time soon.

Anahera spoke to him, her tone reassuring and her touch intended to calm, but Luke could see that they needed help. Drugs that would take control of whatever abnormal things were going on in Tane's brain.

He'd seen many patients like this but having to deal with what was clearly very serious in a remote island village was alarming. Anahera was taking it in stride, however. At her direction, the young woman who was probably Tane's wife had produced a bowl of water and a cloth and was sponging him to try and bring his temperature down. Thankfully, the dreadful shouting and distressed movements stopped as Tane seemed to be overtaken by exhaustion. His head fell back on the woven bedding and his eyes drifted closed. That was when Anahera looked up and caught Luke's gaze.

'Are you thinking what I'm thinking?'

'Encephalitis?' Luke nodded grimly. 'Can you find out if he's had a mosquito bite recently?'

Anahera's face fell as she listened to the people around her. 'There's been a lot more mosquitoes around recently,' she relayed to Luke. 'Lots of people have been bitten. We need to get Tane to hospital as soon as possible, don't we?'

Like the cavalry arriving, Jack came running, the resus kit looped over his shoulder and an oxygen cylinder in his hand. Behind him, two of the villagers were carrying a stretcher.

'You'd better take over,' Anahera told Luke. 'You're the expert. Tell me what you need me to do.'

'Let's get fluids up and get some diazepam on board. We'll have to wait till we get back to Wildfire to do the necessary tests, like a lumbar puncture. When we see how well he's maintaining his airway after sedation, we'll know whether we need to intubate.'

Luke crouched beside Anahera as she opened the kit and pulled out the IV kit and drug roll. He took the gloves she handed him and pulled them on. Her movements were swift and competent. She put a tourniquet on Tane's upper arm and swabbed his elbow with an alcohol wipe. Luke had only just finished snapping the latex gloves into place when she peeled open a cannula package and held it out for him.

He hadn't worked in partnership with Anahera like this since he'd left Wildfire Island.

And it felt good.

Better than good.

It felt…right…

As if something that had been broken had been unexpectedly fixed.

CHAPTER FOUR

THE FLIGHT BACK to Wildfire Island was a race against time.

There was so much to do and everything was so urgent that there was no space in Anahera's head to even recall, let alone think about, the bombshell that Luke had dropped in telling her about his wife.

When they got their desperately ill patient to the hospital the pace picked up even more but at least there were extra hands to help and the facilities available were enough to surprise Luke.

'You've got a bench top scanning electron micro-scope?'

'Down in the research centre laboratory.' Sam nod-ded. 'I'm no microbiologist, though. It's more a hobby for me—a programme of self-tuition. I use all the other gear more—to do all the standard blood tests like a full blood count, glucose and electrolytes and things like toxicology screens.'

'I've done more than enough with an electron microscope to recognise a flavivirus in a CSF sam-ple. Thanks, Ana...' Luke picked up the syringe of local anaesthetic from the trolley prepared for the next diagnostic procedure needed.

Anahera stayed to help keep Tane in position for the lumbar puncture, lying on his side with his chin tucked down and his knees bent up. She made sure that there was no disruption to his IV fluids or oxygen supply and then listened to the conversation between Sam and Luke.

'We'll start him on acyclovir until we can rule out herpes simplex.'

'And antibiotics? What about meningitis or a brain abscess?'

'We'll do a CT next. Can't believe you've got CT capability now. It's a huge advantage. I wouldn't want to be waiting for a plane to get here from Australia.'

'Must still seem limited to what you have on hand in London.'

'It's enough. It's not as if we've got anything more than supportive treatment for any forms of encephalitis other than herpes simplex.' Luke glanced up as he waited for the drops of clear cerebrospinal fluid to drip into the test tube. 'You happy with ICU protocols for managing a case like this, Ana?'

Her nod was confident. 'I'll get the head of the bed elevated thirty degrees and keep the room quiet and not brightly lit. Daily fluids need to be dropped to three quarters of routine maintenance. I'll keep a close eye on any signs of increasing intracranial pressure with vital sign monitoring and if we need to intubate, I can monitor the ventilation. I'll stay in tonight—I just need to give my mother a call and let her know I won't be home.'

Luke turned to Sam. 'You've got other nurses available, haven't you?'

'No one has Ana's ICU experience. And no one

has your expertise in managing an encephalitis case.' Sam pressed on the puncture site as Luke removed the needle from Tane's back. 'I hope you're not planning on leaving any time soon?'

One corner of Luke's mouth curled up. 'I think I'll be here for a bit longer. Unfinished business...'

Anahera focussed on keeping Tane's oxygen mask in place as they rolled him onto his back but her heart skipped a beat. Was she included in what Luke had meant by that cryptic comment?

But Sam was nodding. 'Yeah...Jack said you hadn't even got near one of the hibiscus bushes to collect your bark samples. I guess we'll have to get you out to French Island again.' He clicked the side rails of the bed into place. 'Do you want to take the CSF and blood samples down to the lab? I'll have the CT scan done by the time you're back.'

Anahera watched Luke leave. Sam was happy enough with his interpretation of Luke's 'unfinished business' but she was quite sure that the research into M'Langi tea was only part of it.

The bigger part was the unfinished business of a relationship that had gone so very wrong.

And it seemed that the blame for that could be laid squarely at her own feet. Not only was she guilty in having made a judgement without knowing the facts, she had just made things a whole lot worse by lying to Luke.

She hadn't really lied, had she?

It was the early hours of the morning now and Anahera was sitting beside Tane's bed, listening to the soft beep of the cardiac monitor and watching the rise and fall of her patient's chest.

Sam and Luke were in the staffroom, hopefully catching a little sleep on the comfortable reclining chairs. Hettie was here to help with the nursing but there were other patients that needed care, and Tane couldn't be left alone, so Anahera's offer to stay on had been appreciated.

She had seen respect in Luke's expression when she'd offered to take on the intensive nursing. Admiration, even.

He wouldn't look at her like that if he knew…

Lying by omission was still lying, wasn't it? It was the trick to lying convincingly, wasn't it, to make sure that there was an element of truth in the lie. Of course Luke had believed her. It was true that Hana's father was a doctor. That she'd been born in Brisbane. And that there'd never been any chance of a relationship with her father.

Except there had been, hadn't there?

She'd been there when Vailea had come in with the shocking message that his wife was asking for him back in London, and her reaction had been instant and damning.

She'd turned her back on Luke and walked away, without giving him any chance to say anything.

And she'd done it again when he'd tracked her down and phoned her in Brisbane. When she'd known she was pregnant and it could have made all the difference in the world if she'd given him the chance to tell her the truth.

Instead, she'd gone through her pregnancy and the birth of her baby alone. All those struggles of coping with a new baby by herself. Of not knowing whether she'd been doing the right thing and the fear that something was really wrong when there hadn't seemed to be any way to comfort her infant. Those awful moments of misery when she'd simply been too tired to cope and had had to keep going without anyone there to encourage or reassure her.

Surely that had been punishment enough for her mistake?

No. Thanks to her deception today, there would be more punishment to come if she did tell Luke the truth.

He had been honest with her and he deserved the same respect in return, but the implications of reciprocating were so huge she couldn't begin to get her head around them.

Her life—and those of the people she loved more than life itself—would change for ever.

It would also destroy any trust that Luke had in her.

And that mattered more than she wanted to admit.

As if her patient was aware of the tension building inside Anahera, a grimace appeared on his face and then the muscles of his body seemed to shrink and stiffen. Within the few seconds of registering what was happening, Tane was once again in the throes of a seizure. Anahera hit the alarm button on the wall, which she knew would sound in the staffroom, and then did her best to stop IV lines tangling or pulling free from the forceful jerking of Tane's arms.

It was Luke who came into the room.

'How long has he been seizing again?'

'About a minute.'

'Have you given another dose of diazepam?'

'No.' Was Luke disappointed with her performance already? 'I've been trying to secure the IV lines. I didn't have enough hands…'

'Of course you didn't.' The flash of Luke's smile wiped out any impression that he had been criticising her. He reached for a drug ampoule and syringe. 'We'll add in some phenobarbitone.'

Anahera turned her head to glance at the monitor as an alarm sounded. 'His oxygen saturation is dropping.'

Luke nodded, glancing up as he injected the drug. 'We need to get effective control of his airway and then I can juggle meds to see if we can stop the intracranial pressure rising any further.'

'Do you want me to set up for an RSI?'

Luke nodded again. 'Do you think we can manage that on our own? Sam and Hettie are a bit tied up with a baby that's come in with bronchiolitis and is in quite severe respiratory distress.'

Anahera caught Luke's gaze again and held it for a moment. Ideally, a rapid sequence intubation procedure needed a team of three people, an assistant to the person in charge of the airway and someone to manage the drugs. A clear memory surfaced of how well she and Luke had worked together in the past. Could they still do that?

It felt like nothing had changed.

'No problem,' she said. 'I'll set up.'

She worked swiftly, moving a suction unit, having checked that it worked, and then exchanging Tane's oxygen mask for nasal prongs that would keep oxygen running while they worked on securing his airway. Then she unrolled a pack on the top of a trolley, revealing the range of endotracheal tubes, stylets, airways and the laryngoscope and blades that would be needed.

The new medications had controlled Tane's seizure so they had a window of time that would make intubation easier. Luke already had the extra drugs lined up.

'You good to go?'

'When you are.'

'Got a cric kit there?'

The need to create a surgical airway by a cricothyrotomy was an emergency backup in case the intubation attempt was unsuccessful and they had a still paralyzed patient who had no way of breathing for himself. Anahera nodded but then caught Luke's gaze.

'You won't need it.'

Luke maintained the eye contact long enough for Anahera to get the message that he had just as much confidence in her own skills and, despite how critical the next few minutes were going to be, she felt herself relax.

It was still there—that professional connection that had made them such an amazing team.

Luke's focus was completely on the task ahead the instant he looked away. 'Let's pre-oxygenate.'

The procedure went like clockwork. During the three minutes of pre-oxygenation the equipment, drug dosages and monitoring were all checked. Sedation and then the paralysing drugs were administered. Luke obtained visualisation of the vocal cords easily and the tube to secure Tane's airway was slipped into position. Luke's focus was still a hundred per cent on their patient at this point, as he confirmed the correct positioning of the tube by listening to Tane's chest. Anahera's tasks of securing the tube and attaching it to the ventilator were automatic enough for her to find her focus shifting somewhat.

To the doctor rather than the patient.

This wasn't the first time they'd worked together. It wasn't the first time they'd been alone, doing something that had the potential to go wrong with disastrous consequences for the patient either, but it *felt* like the first time.

Anahera's instincts had told her that their professional rapport was still there but she'd forgotten how it actually felt to work with someone where there was such a smooth professional connection it was like one person having an extra pair of hands. She'd never experienced it with anyone else, including all the intensive care specialists she'd worked with in that huge Brisbane hospital. Was it just Luke? Did he achieve that kind of rapport with whoever was assisting him?

Maybe not. He looked away from the ventilator settings and caught her gaze.

'I always knew you were good,' he said quietly. 'But you've even better now. That was a real pleasure.'

The praise sparked a glow of warmth and then Anahera remembered that this was Luke praising her and something weird happened inside her chest—as if a plug had been jarred loose and a leak had sprung from what had been a tight seal. A leak that rapidly turned into a small torrent of…feelings.

The feelings she had once had for Luke that made his praise so much more than professional approval or respect.

Was it even possible to stop loving someone you had once felt so strongly about?

Apparently not. Not in her case, at least…

She had to tear her gaze away from Luke's. Had to move. If she could walk she would feel the ground beneath her feet and it would dispel the alarming sensation that the foundations of the life she had built for herself were not in the process of crumbling. Unfortunately, it seemed that her brain and her body weren't quite in sync and she almost stumbled. Luke's hand caught her arm and steadied her.

'Whoa… You okay, Ana?'

The touch of his hand would have been quite enough to make things worse but it came with the sound of her name and a tone of genuine concern that made her want to cry.

She pulled in a ragged breath but no words emerged.

'You're exhausted,' Luke said quietly. 'Things are under control here now. I'm going to review meds and sedation and then I'll see if Hettie's free to come and cover for you. You need some rest.'

It wasn't rest that Anahera needed as much as some space. Distance from Luke so that she could get that emotional plug securely back where it belonged. She closed her eyes and drew on a strength she hadn't known she possessed.

'I'm fine,' she said. 'I just need a bit of fresh air. I'll stay until the day shift gets here. I…I'll go and sit in the garden for a minute.'

She had always loved it that the three wings of Wildfire Island's hospital were U-shaped and surrounded a lush patch of tropical garden that had a pond and more than one space to sit comfortably and enjoy the serenity and delicious scents of the flowering plants like frangipani and jasmine. At night it took on a life of its own, with pale blooms shining like stars amongst dark green foliage and the chorus of the tiny frogs that called the pond home. The relaxing sound of the trickle of the water feeding the pond was a bonus that wasn't heard in the daytime, thanks to the bustle of people and birdlife.

It was deliciously cool, too. Anahera sat close to the pond and breathed in the last of the night air. The light was also beginning to change and a new day was about to begin. A new day in the life she had chosen for herself and her precious child. And with every breath she reminded herself that this was home and they were safe. Nothing had to change unless she wanted it to.

The frogs falling silent warned her that she wasn't alone any more, even before she heard the rustle of leaves as shrubs were brushed and the sound of approaching feet on the path. It had to be Luke—unless he'd told someone else to come and find her.

She kept her eyes closed as she registered the sounds and even a change in the air as someone sat down on the bench beside her, but she knew she had been right. She had no need to open her eyes to confirm who it was. How weird was that—to recognise someone so easily without seeing them or hearing their voice? Even more astonishing was to feel as though she was more present herself because of having him in the same space. More…alive…

'You okay?'

The query was soft and that concern that had almost been her undoing was still there. Anahera knew she had to open her eyes. If she didn't, he would touch her again to see if she was all right and she couldn't afford to let that happen.

But when she opened her eyes, it was to find Luke

looking directly into them with an expression that told her she was the only thing in the world that mattered to him at this moment.

The way he'd looked at Tane when his patient's life had been his only focus.

The way he'd looked at her once, so long ago, just before he'd kissed her for the very first time.

Any intention to reassure him about her well-being died on her lips. Anahera could only stare back at him. At his eyes and then at his lips as the memory of that first kiss ambushed her head and then took her heart captive.

Maybe those memories were written on her face somehow. Or maybe it was some kind of telepathy.

Whatever it was, the hands of some invisible clock were whirring backwards, faster and faster, taking them both back in time.

It wasn't dawn any more. It was sunset. They weren't sitting on a wooden bench in a well-kept tropical garden. They were standing on a beach with soft sand beneath their bare feet.

And Luke had touched her face—just like this—his fingertips tracing the line of her cheek and jaw as if they were the most beautiful sculpture on earth. With just a single fingertip he brushed her lower lip so gently it felt like the whisper of a butterfly's wing and that was when Anahera knew how lost she was.

Lost in time.

Lost in love.

This kiss was as inevitable as the rising of the sun behind the mountains of this island but Anahera didn't see that first real glow of its appearance because she had closed her eyes again the moment Luke's lips touched her own and then she was aware of nothing but the pleasure of his touch.

A feeling of coming home after the longest journey would have been more than enough to deal with, but that wasn't enough for her body. Or her heart.

Pleasure escalated into desire.

She wanted more.

She *needed* more.

The force of that desire was so shocking she had to pull back and break the contact.

Instinct was telling her to run. To get away before she lost that unexpected strength she'd been able to tap into when she'd realised her feelings for Luke hadn't changed. But the commands her brain was issuing were being totally ignored by her body. She couldn't move. She couldn't even take a breath.

Anahera was trapped by Luke's hands that were still gently cradling her head. By the way he was still looking at her. By the way his breath was released in a poignant sigh.

'Oh, Ana… Nothing's changed, has it?'

CHAPTER FIVE

LUKE REALISED HE couldn't have been more wrong the moment the words left his lips.

Everything had changed.

The way Anahera had responded to his kiss told him something she had been keeping so well hidden, maybe she hadn't even realised it herself.

It was still there—that astonishing connection he'd never known could even exist between two people.

A connection that had brought them together in the first place, professionally and then personally, to explode into an emotional force that made the word *love* seem too small to encompass.

Or maybe she still didn't realise it. Or didn't want to admit it.

She shook her head just enough to dislodge the touch of his hands and she looked as though she wanted to turn and run but she was frozen—her huge, dark eyes filled with something that made his heart want to break.

Fear?

Yes…the flash of what looked like enormous relief a moment later confirmed that awful impression. Someone was calling her name.

Rescue was at hand.

'Ana? You out there? Have you seen Luke?'

He could help her, too. Give her a few moments of peace to realise that she was, in fact, safe. That he would never do anything to hurt her.

Not again…

'I'm here, Sam.' Standing up and moving onto the path that led to the pond made him visible. 'I was just catching a breath of fresh air. What's up?'

Turning his head, he could see that Anahera was going to accept the gift of privacy, but the way she had buried her face in her hands was just as heartbreaking as the fear he had seen in her eyes.

This was no fairy-tale reunion, then, with the glow of a happy-ever-after lighting the way forward.

But it *was* something that needed resolution. If things were left like this it was clearly going to haunt them both, probably for the rest of their lives. And Luke already knew the damaging effects that could have because he'd been living with it for nearly five years.

People used the term 'the love of my life' all the time but it was only in recent years that Luke had come to understand what it really meant. Yes, there were many, many people in the world that you could be compatible with. Could love, in fact, and go on to have a very happy life in their company, but, for some people, there was one who stood on a different level and if you were lucky enough to connect with them, nothing would ever be the same.

For Luke, that person was Anahera. Every time he thought of her—and barely a day went past in his life when something, however tiny, didn't remind him—

the thought was accompanied by a sense of loss. Of losing something that he knew he would never find again because…well, because Anahera was the love of his life.

And maybe…just maybe—despite the devastating evidence to the contrary that she'd had a child with another man—Anahera's life had been affected as well. She wasn't with the father of her child any more, was she?

It took a moment to tune in to what Sam was saying.

'…so I thought if you took the morning meeting and briefed the day staff, you could get some sleep. I'll give you a pager and we can send a driver if there's any deterioration in Tane's condition. Or we can find a bed in the hospital for you to crash on.'

'That would be better. The next twenty-four hours are going to be critical. Maybe longer. How did you go with getting the chest X-ray?'

'That's what I wanted to show you. You were right about those crackles in both lung fields. There's bilateral pulmonary oedema.'

Luke nodded grimly as he followed Sam down the corridor. 'I suspect his pulmonary status is going to get worse. If it develops into ARDS, we're looking at a week or more of intensive care before we can expect any improvement.'

'Should we consider evacuating him?'

'There's no point. All that can be done is supportive measures and we can do that here. This way, he'll at least have his family nearby.'

'We? Are you saying you'll stay that long?'

'I'll contact my department later today. As far as I

know, I don't have anything in my diary that couldn't be handled by my senior staff and…and I could do with a bit more time. We need to set up that research project and I haven't collected those tea-leaves yet.'

He had another reason to want more time and that it was personal rather than professional failed to make it any less important. That kiss had changed something huge. An unspoken rule that Luke had been living by for far too long had just been exposed as being un-founded in truth. Work wasn't more important than anything else life had to offer and it wasn't the only route to happiness or fulfilment. It may have been a successful strategy to bury himself in his profession to the extent that he could ignore every other aspect of his life but he couldn't do that any longer.

Not after *that* kiss.

He knew it might be one of the hardest things he'd ever had to do, but somehow he had to find a way to talk about this with Anahera. Really talk, openly and honestly. And the hardest thing about that was likely to be getting Anahera to agree to have that talk.

In the meantime, burying anything personal by fo-cussing totally on the welfare of someone who desper-ately needed his professional expertise was not only vital but a retreat into a comfort zone he really needed right now.

The sun was almost halfway visible above the moun-tains by the time Anahera removed the shelter of her hands and exposed her face to the world again.

Good grief…how long had she been sitting there like a stunned rabbit, unable to break the spell of that kiss or to move herself from being trapped beneath the weight of that onslaught of long-buried feelings?

Not to mention the shock of what had seemed so blindingly obvious in the silent communication of that kiss. Even if Luke hadn't said that nothing had changed, she would have known that he still wanted her. Still loved her?

No. She tried to shake that thought away. She had been the one who'd been head over heels in love and dreaming of a future. If what was between them had been strong enough for Luke to have intended keeping her in his life, surely he would have told her about the little complication that his *wife* represented?

The flash of anger was almost a welcome addition to the kaleidoscope of emotions because it was so very familiar. Anahera had relied on it as a way through the heartbreak of what had been an ultimate betrayal.

It didn't feel quite the same now, though. It had lost its power because she knew the truth.

What could she hang on to now as a framework to make such big decisions about the future?

'*Ana*...they said I might find you out here.' Her mother's face creased with concern. 'You look... You haven't been crying, have you?'

'Oh, Mum.' It was such a comfort to have her mother sit on the bench beside her and to be folded into the arms that had always made anything so much easier to bear. 'It's been quite a night.'

'So I heard. Tane's very sick, isn't he?'

'I'm afraid so.'

'His family are on the way to sit with him. I'm going to make sure we've got enough food for every-body.' Vailea sighed. 'I wish there was more I could do to help. At least we're lucky enough to have a world expert in treating encephalitis here.'

'Luke won't be here for long, Mum. He'll have to get back to his work in London.'

'Hettie tells me he's put off going back so he can look after Tane. And it's even more important that the research gets going so that we don't have more cases like this in the future. He's a wonderful man, isn't he?'

'Mmm.' The sound was choked. The emotional cauldron Anahera was immersed in had just been stirred again. She felt ridiculously proud of Luke for putting his own life on hold to help Tane. There was a wash of relief that he wouldn't be walking out of her life in the immediate future but there were also newly sharpened edges to the guilt and a deepened dread of the consequences if she told him the truth.

It was all too much. She wanted to bury her face against her mother's neck and stop trying to hold back her tears. She wanted to tell her everything and ask for advice but she already knew what her mother would say. Vailea had been horrified that Hana's father had apparently walked out of their lives and had never wanted contact with his child. She couldn't understand how any parent could do that. How disappointed would she be with her own daughter if she found out that it was Anahera who had forced that lack of contact?

So she choked back the tears and pulled herself out of the embrace that had the potential to weaken her resolve and turn their lives upside down before she was ready to do that herself. At least she had a small reprieve of time to choose when—or if—she was ready.

'How's Hana? Did she miss me last night?'

'Of course. But she's learned to take times like this

in her stride.' Vailea smiled. 'She's such a happy little soul. I took her up to Bessie at the house, and she
danced up the path, flapping her arms. Said she was
being a flutterby today.'

Anahera's smile wobbled and she couldn't stop a
tear escaping. And then another one.

'Tch…' Vailea smoothed the tears away with her
thumb. 'You're just too tired, darling. Hana's fine.
Bessie loves her as much as we do. She's safe and
happy and she'll be even happier when she sees her
mumma later. What you need is some sleep. And some
food. When did you last have something to eat?'

'I…I guess it was the sandwiches you made for us
to take to French Island for the clinic run yesterday.'

Vailea's huff of sound was appalled. 'Come with
me. I'm going to whip up some scrambled eggs for
you. You can't sleep properly on such an empty stomach. And then you can go home.'

'I need to talk to Sam and see what the roster is like.
We're going to need extra staff for the next few days.
Tane will have to have someone with him at all times
and I'm the only nurse with intensive care training.'

'You can talk to him while you're having your
breakfast. I'll make sure those doctors come and eat
as well.'

Breakfast with Luke? Knowing that every time she
looked at his face she would be remembering that kiss?
Falling back into the whirlpool of the feelings that had
surfaced? She couldn't do it. Not yet. The thought of
having to try was disturbing enough to push Anahera
to her feet.

'I'll tell Sam you're making breakfast but I'll find
something at home. Or I'll pick a mango or pawpaw

on the way. I'm so tired I think I'd be sick if I tried to eat something hot.'

Vailea simply nodded and smiled. 'I'll have something ready for you when you get back.'

Their paths diverged as they entered the covered walkway between the hospital rooms and the garden.

'Sleep well, my love,' Vailea said by way of farewell. 'Love you…'

'Love you, too.'

Anahera needed to turn right to go in search of Sam, who would either be with Tane or in the staff-room, but, for a long moment, she watched the tall figure and straight back of her mother as she headed towards the kitchens.

She had always had something ready for her. Food, shelter, acceptance, love…

Anahera barely remembered her father, even though there were plenty of photographs and she'd been told so often that her daddy loved her.

Exhaustion took on a peaceful edge suddenly and the whirlpool stopped spinning.

She didn't need anger any more. She could use logic as a framework, along with the evidence that her own history provided. Parents that belonged in different worlds couldn't forge a family no matter how much they might want to. She could use her head instead of her heart.

How selfish would it be to put her own needs or desires ahead of those of her child? Or her mother, for that matter, when Vailea was still devoting her life to her daughter and her granddaughter?

So she still loved Luke. And maybe he still wanted her. But the love story, if that was what it was, had been doomed before it had even begun. The best thing for everybody would be to close the book and walk away.

And maybe that was the answer. If she could persuade herself that those things were all that needed to be said, they might be able to part on good terms—with a clean slate to begin the rest of their lives. Okay, so her slate wouldn't be completely clean, but in a way, she would be telling him *why* she couldn't tell him the truth and that could—hopefully—make that lump of guilt a bit easier to live with.

She just needed to find an opportunity to talk to him.

Luke had known that finding an opportunity to even suggest a private talk to Anahera would be difficult, but he hadn't bargained on it being impossible.

In the few hours she had gone home to sleep, members of Tane's family and community began to arrive and fill spaces in and around the hospital and any free moments for any member of staff were taken up with making sure these people were kept informed and offered all the support they needed.

Given the available space and the need for such intensive monitoring, only one person at a time, other than his wife, Kura, could be allowed to sit with Tane, and these people were all frightened. They were listening to every beep of the monitors and watching everything that was done, desperately waiting for any sign that would give them hope.

The atmosphere was sombre. Knowing that Tane's eight-month-old son was among the family members being cared for outside the intensive care unit added to the tension. When Anahera arrived back at the hospital in the early afternoon, Luke was with Tane, adjusting the parameters of the ventilator again. Kura was on a chair pressed against the head of the bed, her hand touching Tane's cheek, and his mother, Marama, was standing behind Kura, her hands resting on the young mother's shoulders. They watched Hettie slip out of the room to allow Anahera to take her place, and Luke could feel the intensity of the way they waited for Luke to greet her.

Even a meaningful glance between the doctor and nurse, who understood far more than the family could, had the potential to be easily misinterpreted, which might add to the suffering of the people who loved this young man in their care. But Luke already knew that and he was an expert in shutting anything remotely personal out of the professional sphere. That only hours ago kissing this woman had shaken his world so hard it was still rattling was irrelevant. His greeting was no different than it would have been if Sam had come into the room and eye contact no more than polite.

Thankfully, Anahera was clearly in exactly the same space. She moved close enough to brush his shoulder but her gaze was on the ventilator settings and her swift glance showed that she recognised the significance of every change he'd just made.

The glance hadn't gone unnoticed.

'What's wrong?' Kura whispered. 'Is he getting worse?'

'His breathing is getting harder for him.' Anahera slipped past Luke to touch Kura's hand. 'We can help by changing the settings on the machine, like how much oxygen we give him and what the pressure needs to be to get it right into his lungs.'

Both women looked bewildered, and Anahera switched languages. After answering many questions, the women nodded and turned their attention back to Tane. Anahera stepped back.

'It was harder than I thought it would be to explain positive end expiratory pressure and how it helps to increase it.' A line appeared between her eyes as she scanned Luke's face. 'Have you had any sleep?'

'Not yet.' That Anahera clearly cared how he was did something weird to Luke's heart, as if it was filling up with a physiologically impossible amount of blood that was warmer than it should be as it got pumped to every cell in his body.

'Where's Sam?'

'Doing a round of the other inpatients. I don't think he's slept yet either.'

She was still holding his gaze. This might seem like no more than a professional exchange to anyone around them but it *was* more. So much more. They were more than simply a team working as a single unit towards the same goal. The bond was laced with concern. A tenderness that offered hope for the future?

'I'll hold the fort in here. Just bring me up to speed.'

'I've charted all the drugs here.' Luke picked up the chart on the end of Tane's bed. 'The lorazepam and morphine seem to be enough to be keeping him comfortable and maintaining ventilator synchrony. His temperature is stable but I'd like to see it come down further.'

'I'll give him a sponge bath. That's something that

Kura will be able to help with. I'll show them how to massage his hands and feet, too.'

Luke nodded. The more they could involve Tane's family in his care, the better. It was no surprise that Anahera would already be planning how to do that. How to care for every member of his family as well as her patient. Everything she did was tinged with the extraordinary amount of love she had to offer.

Was her concern for him purely because he was in her orbit right now? That curious warmth in his body had faded enough that he knew he would probably dismiss it later as a combination of tiredness and imagination.

'I want to get another chest X-ray in a few hours. We'll need to put in a gastric tube for enteral feeding but that can wait a little while, too.'

It was Anahera's turn to nod. 'Until you're rested.' She was already turning back to her patient. 'I'll call you if anything changes.'

Luke almost smiled as he left the room. He'd been dismissed but he was happy enough to go. He'd be no use to anyone unless he got some sleep. Maybe he had imagined the secret level he and Anahera had been communicating on for a few seconds there but he had absolutely no doubt that she could—and would—provide the best care that Tane needed.

Tragically, even the best care wasn't going to be enough for this young islander. Tane's condition deteriorated slowly over the next twenty-four hours and, early the next afternoon, his heart gave up the struggle and stopped. The desperate attempts of the medical team were unsuccessful in getting it started again and the ventilator was finally switched off when his family could return to surround his bed. Even his small baby was silent in his mother's arms as the final impression of life faded.

The whole hospital fell silent as the news spread and people gathered to comfort each other. And then the tears began. Luke was close to tears himself as people came up to him to thank him for everything he'd done. The generosity of their gratitude in the face of his failure was overwhelming, and the grief was contagious.

He had failed. And it hurt.

'Get some rest, mate…' Sam's grip on his shoulder was tight. 'We'll take care of everything here.'

Anahera was right behind Sam. She had Tane's baby in her arms and the pain of failure got a whole lot sharper. They'd not only lost a young man in the prime of his life; a wife had lost her husband and a baby had lost his father. Pain morphed into anger. Not at himself, because he knew he'd done everything any doctor could have done—this anger was at the unfairness of life and the suffering dealt out to people who had done nothing to deserve it.

'The family want to take Tane home,' Anahera said. 'I'll help get him ready. We'll need the death certificate filled in…' She hesitated and bit her lip, her gaze barely touching Luke's.

'I'll do that,' Sam said quietly. 'We just need you to sign it.'

Luke's nod was grim. 'Just show me where the forms are. I'll do it.' He had been the physician in charge of the case and this was his responsibility. 'And then I'll get out of everybody's way. There's nothing more for me to do here.' He shook his head. He couldn't keep a lid on his anger any more and he had to let some of it out. 'I'd better see how soon I can book a flight back to London. No reason not to head back tomorrow if it's possible.'

Anahera's shocked intake of breath was overtaken by the wail of the baby she was holding, which was probably why Sam didn't notice, but Luke heard it, and it cut through him like a knife.

He'd lost control of his anger but he hadn't intended directing it towards Anahera.

He could see exactly how she was interpreting his words in the way her eyes darkened and the frozen expression on her face. He was telling her that she wasn't a reason to want to be here. That he didn't want any more to do with her.

For a heartbeat Luke stayed where he was. He even opened his mouth to say something that would mollify his dismissal of his time here, but nothing came out. The baby was sobbing now, and Luke could see the grandmother, Marama, coming towards them. She would probably smile at Luke and add to the number of people thanking him for the care he'd taken of Tane.

He couldn't take any more of it. Any of it. What was the point of trying to talk to Anahera anyway? The kind of conversation he'd had in mind was a minefield of making yourself vulnerable and then having to deal with pain, and he'd had more than enough of that today.

It was far easier to turn on his heel and follow Sam, who was already moving towards the office where the grim paperwork would need to be completed, so that was exactly what Luke did.

CHAPTER SIX

So that was it?

Luke was simply going to turn his back on Wildfire Island—and *her*—and ride off into the sunset without a backward glance?

Talk about hitting someone when they were already down.

Tears flowed freely as Anahera worked with Kura and Marama to prepare Tane's body to be returned to his home and the churchyard where he would be buried within a few days.

She removed the tracheal tube, the IV lines and ECG electrodes as carefully as if her patient could still feel every touch. She brought scented water and warm, fluffy towels so that Tane's wife and mother could bathe him. She listened to the traditional, soft songs of grief and her heart broke a little more with every verse.

The undertaker had been summoned, and Tane would have to be in his care for a while before his final voyage back to his own island. Anahera joined the solemn procession of family and friends to accompany his body to the boat. Sam walked by her side, but Luke was nowhere to be seen.

'He's taken it hard,' Sam said quietly. 'I suspect he's got used to saving people even when they get to a critical stage. From what I hear, that's what he did for that sheikh—Harry—who's poured a fortune into developing the new vaccine. It's a personal failure for him.'

'It's personal for all of us. These are *our* people.'

'They are.'

His glance reminded Anahera that Sam had no island blood in his veins. He had been born and raised in Britain—like Luke—but he never talked about his old life except to say he was happy to have left it behind. This young doctor had virtually washed up on the shores of these islands and then had never left, but even if it hadn't been so long ago, he would be one of her people. There was something about him that meant he had been one of them from the moment he'd arrived.

'Is he really going to leave tomorrow?'

'I've asked him not to. He thinks we can sort all the details of setting up the clinical trial for the new vaccine by internet connection but...' Sam shook his head. 'I get the feeling he needs to be here longer for his own sake as much as mine.'

Anahera's heart skipped a beat. Had Luke said something? About *her*? About his 'unfinished business'?

They stood a little apart as Tane's immediate family said their temporary farewells until they could have their loved one with them again. A heart-rending wail from Kura split the air as the undertaker's boat pushed off from the jetty.

'We have to do all we can to make sure this doesn't happen again,' Sam said, his voice raw. 'And that's the way forward for us all. A way to deal with the grief and any sense of failure. I don't want Luke to go off and carry this on his own shoulders. He saved Harry and he was there when the whole concept of developing the vaccine started. Actually being here himself to set up and start the trial would give him something a whole lot more positive to take away from here.'

It should have been a relief to hear that Sam had no knowledge of a personal past history and that he thought any benefit to Luke staying longer had a professional basis. It should have been a relief that she might not have to make that decision of whether or not to talk to Luke and what to tell him when she did, because the moment his plane took off, her life would go back to exactly what it had been.

Anahera was nodding but yet another piece of her heart was breaking. This wasn't right. Of course Sam had intuitively picked up that there was something Luke badly needed to heal his life that he would only find here. He just didn't know that it had a whole lot more to do with her than this tragic case he had inadvertently taken responsibility for.

But what on earth could she do about it?

'You okay?' Sam pulled her into the kind of hug only a brother or a very good friend could provide. 'It's been a rough couple of days.'

'I think I need a walk, that's all. A bit of quiet time to sort my head out. I might go and watch the sunset.'

'The tide's out. You could walk around to Sunset Beach from here and get the best view of all.'

'Sounds like a good idea.'

Or not. Sunset Beach had been the place she and

Luke had shared their first ever kiss. Where they'd made love for the first time.

'Can I do anything? Want me to pick Hana up and look after her for a while?' Sam's smile was crooked. 'I love time with kids. I reckon that's all I need to sort *my* head out.'

'Mum will have already gone to do that. She had almost finished packing up the extra food to send back with Tane's family when I talked to her before we left the hospital.' Anahera returned his smile. 'But go and visit. Take Bugsy with you.'

Bugsy was a gorgeous golden retriever who belonged to Maddie—one of the FIFO doctors—and Sam looked after her on Maddie's regular weeks back on the mainland. 'Mum would love to see you, and Hana adores Bugsy. And her uncle Sam. Like every other kid on these islands.'

Her smile faded. In the years that Sam had been here she'd never seen any sign of him wanting to find a relationship. Would he ever have children of his own to spend time with?

Would Luke go on to find someone else and have a child he could knowingly call his own?

What if he didn't and she was depriving him of the kind of joy she had been blessed to have ever since Hana had been born?

'I might do that.' But Sam was frowning. 'Bugsy needs a walk. But are you sure you don't want some company? You look…'

'I'm fine.' Anahera's interruption was swift. If he said anything else, she might burst into tears and confess everything. 'Or I will be. Tell Mum that for me, will you? And not to worry if I'm not home for a bit.'

* * *

Sunset Beach was the only place Anahera could go
to watch the sunset given how close it was as the last
of Tane's family piled onto the ferry that would take
them home. To one side of the harbour was the rocky
promontory with the church on top, and the only way
round was the road that led to the village. The beaches
on that side would have groups of children shouting
and splashing in the calm water sheltered by the reef
and she really didn't want company right now. Far
better to pick her way past the rock pools exposed by
the low tide to get to the beach with the shadow of the
cliffs beside her that would catch fire as the sun said
its goodbye for the day.

She took her sandals off as soon as she was past
the rock pools to feel the sand beneath her feet and
paused again, a moment later, to pull the fastening off
the end of her long plait and unravel her hair so that it
could flow down her back and get ruffled by the delicious sea breeze.

This was exactly what she needed. To be alone and
immerse herself in the elements. The sound of the
gentle waves breaking and the leaves of palm trees
rustling overhead, the smell of salt mixed with the
sweetness of unseen flowers and the caress of the sun's
warmth made perfect by the cool breeze.

Anahera could centre herself here. She could let
herself become one with the beauty surrounding her
and realise what a microscopic piece of the universe
she—and her problems—represented. Maybe some of
those worries would simply ebb away with the pull of
each wave and they would be diluted by the vastness
of this ocean that cradled her home.

She watched the waves and then looked past where they were breaking to where the water changed from turquoise to a deep blue. It was only then that she saw the swimmer. Someone who was swimming hard and fast, as though they were trying to wash away whatever demons were chasing them.

It could have been anyone, but Anahera knew instantly that it was Luke. Of course it was. The exclusive bures built for the new conference and research facility were just around the rock fall at the other end of Sunset Beach. Had some part of her agreed with Sam's suggestion of a destination because she'd known there was a chance of her path crossing Luke's?

It didn't matter. She was here now and this had been meant to happen.

She had to shade her eyes from the sun as it dipped lower and it made it increasingly hard to see the movement in the water, but she stayed exactly where she was and simply waited. The cliffs behind her were turning a spectacular blood red as the dark shape finally emerged from the shallows, and even though the light behind him made it impossible to read Luke's expression, Anahera could tell the moment he saw her by the way he stopped—as though he'd walked into a brick wall.

And then he started walking again.

Towards her.

Anahera's heart picked up speed. She tried to remember what it was she had wanted to tell him when they got a chance to talk but it was scrambling in her head. Something about her parents. About not repeating history...

But here they were, alone on Sunset Beach, and

that was repeating a history that was making Ana-hera's legs feel like jelly and making rational thought increasingly impossible.

She had no idea how she was even going to greet Luke, let alone say anything of any significance.

She didn't need to say anything. Luke came close and his smile said it all. He knew exactly why she had come here. Why she had needed to. His single word summed it up.

'Better?'

She nodded. 'You?'

He mirrored her nod. 'I'm sorry.'

'What for?' Anahera held his gaze. She couldn't let it fall because he was standing so close to her and he was virtually naked, droplets of sea water proba-bly clinging to every inch of that smooth, olive skin. The shiver she had to repress had nothing to do with the sea breeze.

'The way I left. What I said. Sam was right. I can't walk away yet. I've got to get this trial set up. It oc-curred to me while I was swimming that we're going to have to comb every record of encephalitis cases on the island so we've got statistics to use as a measure for how effective the vaccine is. It's a massive job, and I'll have to show Sam how to carry it on when I've gone. The data entry and so forth...' Luke pushed his wet hair back from his face. 'And then there's the tea-leaves. I still need samples but that made me think, too. If it's got any use against the mosquitoes and the bushes grow on French Island, why did Tane get bit-ten?'

Knowing that Luke wasn't going to vanish from her life immediately was like taking a huge gulp of a very heady cocktail. There was relief there. And something a whole lot stronger. Like joy?

Anahera had to press her lips together to suppress a smile. Had to focus to remember what it was that Luke had been saying.

'Maybe Tane didn't like the tea.'

'That's something we'll have to find out. That's going to be a whole study in itself. Brrr...' Luke rubbed his arms. 'That swim was cooler than I thought it would be.'

'The sun's almost gone.' Anahera let her gaze drop now. To the soft sand that had encrusted his feet and had been kicked up to stick as far as his knees. Up to swimming shorts that were dripping, past an impressively flat abdomen and then...yes, the water was still clinging, especially to the sprinkle of dark hair on his chest between nipples standing out like tiny pebbles in the chill. Hastily, she returned her gaze to his face.

'Where's your towel?'

'Back at my bure. I kind of forgot.'

'You probably need a shower.'

'What I really need...' Luke wiped a hand across his face but didn't drop the eye contact '...is to talk to you.'

Here it was. The opportunity that had been impossible to find since that time in the hospital garden. They could talk. Part on good terms, even?

Anahera's mouth felt suddenly dry. It was hard to swallow. 'I'll...I'll come with you, then. I don't have to be home for a while.'

There was a moment's silence, long enough to make it clear that Luke was registering the significance of her offer. Long enough for the wash of a wave to be heard, along with a mournful cry of some unseen sea bird.

He didn't say anything but he didn't have to. His nod and that slow smile told her that he welcomed the idea. Maybe that it was more than he had hoped for.

The silence continued as they walked together. Along to the other end of Sunset Beach, as the last of the colour drained from the cliffs towering alongside, leaving the pattern of their footprints in the sand. The tide was still out far enough to make it easy to get around the rock fall at the end of the beach, and within moments they could glimpse the first of the bures that had been built to accommodate the visitors to the conference and research facility.

The smell of the shrubs planted to screen the bures from each other made Anahera draw in an appreciative breath.

Luke smiled. 'It's lovely, isn't it? I'd forgotten the scent of ginger flowers.'

'I haven't seen these bures before. This area has been fenced off for ages. The first time I've been here for years was when Sam and I came down to that doctor we thought was having a heart attack at your conference.'

'Charles.' Luke nodded. 'I had an email from him yesterday. They brought his coronary angiogram forward as soon as he got home. He ended up with three stents to fix his arteries and he reckons he's good for another forty years or so.'

'That's good to hear. He was lucky.'

This was an easy way to break the silence. To talk about people other than themselves.

'He said he wants to come back. I must ask Harry

if they're going to rent out these bures to people who might just want a break. They could make a fortune if they did.'

'Turn it into some kind of resort?' Anahera frowned. 'I don't think the Lockharts would allow that to happen on Wildfire Island. But then, I didn't think they'd lease even part of it like this. I'm sure it was Ian's idea, not Max's.'

'Ian's his brother, isn't he? I seem to remember hearing some opinions about his character that were not very flattering.'

'Nobody likes him. He was the black sheep of the family and was apparently no support at all when Max's wife died and he was struggling to care for the twins. I think he did his best to bleed the family fortune dry even when Max needed so much money to get care for Christopher.'

'Caroline's twin, yes? The one with cerebral palsy.'

'Yes. Max has been living in Australia with him for years. Ian was given the job of running the mine a few years back but Mum says that he was just using the money for himself, probably gambled it away, and then he just took off. The mine's been closed recently because it isn't safe. Ian hasn't been seen for weeks and nobody knows where he is. Caroline came back just last month and she was horrified by how run-down everything's become but she's determined to save the mine and the jobs for everyone.' Anahera turned to follow Luke up a pathway from the beach that led to one of the bures. 'Maybe it's not such a crazy idea, starting a resort.'

Stepping inside the bure, her eyes widened.

'This looks like a resort already. Like something

you only see in a magazine.' Her gaze followed the round walls with the louvred windows, up to the coved ceiling and then down to where the softly draped mosquito nets framed a huge bed made up with crisp-looking white linen. Whoever had serviced the room had sprinkled frangipani blossoms over the cover, which made it look even more inviting.

Romantic, even…

Luke had no idea she was finding it hard to take in a new breath.

'Have a look at the bathroom while I find my clothes. It's astonishing…'

It was. Anahera looked at the bowl on the vanity bench, where a pretty pattern of colourful petals had been left as decoration beside a pile of fluffy white towels. At the design of the fish in the mosaic of the shower floor. At the stone walls and the rainhead fitting. And then she imagined Luke standing in here, naked, under the fall of water, and she had to close her eyes and step back. To lean against the wall for a moment, even.

'Ana? Are you okay?'

She opened her eyes to find Luke standing close. Too close. She could see the tiny flecks of gold and brown that made his eyes hazel more than green. He had some dry clothes in one hand but he was still wearing only his damp swimming shorts, and looking at his face couldn't remove that bare chest in her peripheral vision. It had been manageable out in the open space of the beach, with the sea stretching for ever on one side, but nothing could mitigate the effect of him standing so close, in a confined space, with all that skin within touching distance. She could feel the heat of it. Could smell the salt of the sea and something else that opened an avalanche of memories.

The smell of...Luke...

Anahera opened her mouth to say she was fine. Tensed every muscle in her body that she would need to move. To slip past Luke and into the safety of a larger room.

But nothing happened. No words emerged. No muscle twitched.

And Luke was just as still.

The soft thud of a handful of clothing being discarded barely registered, and the touch of Luke's hand on her face was so intense that she had to close her eyes again. She still hadn't closed her mouth after that abortive attempt to say anything, and it was too late by the time she felt the touch of Luke's lips.

It was too late to talk. To move. To *think*...

'Oh... *Ana*...' The word was almost a prayer. Luke's hands had trailed down her body, over her breasts and then slipped up under the top of her uniform to touch her skin by the time his lips were lifted enough for him to speak. 'Do you want this as much as I do? I can stop...'

The sound that came from Anahera's lips was no more than a whimper of need. She had wanted this for ever. She just hadn't known how much.

It was a tiny sound but it had the effect of unleashing something huge. Luke had the hem of her green tunic in his hands now and he was lifting it. Anahera raised her arms to make it easier to shed the item of clothing that represented a barrier between his skin and hers. It had to go, along with everything else she was wearing. So that Luke could touch her anywhere. Everywhere.

Especially *there*...

Her legs were losing the ability to hold her upright but it didn't matter. Not when there was a pair of strong arms to support her. To scoop her up and carry her and then lay her down amongst the fragrant lemon-and-white blossoms of the frangipani. Blossoms that released even more scent as they were crushed by her body lying on them. Then Luke stepped back, turned and retrieved his wallet from the dressing table. She watched him fumble through it, searching for a condom. He turned to face her, a question in his eyes: *Are we going to do this?*

Nothing needed to be said. They had never needed to ask what was needed or preferred because they had been in tune with each other from that very first time of such gentle, passionate lovemaking. This was nothing like that first time. The sex was hard and fast. Almost desperate—as if they'd both been wanting this for ever. As if they were grabbing something illicit because they knew they might never have another opportunity?

And then they lay facing each other, their faces only inches apart, as they both tried to catch their breath and wait until their hearts stopped racing.

It was Luke who broke the silence.

'I wish I could turn back time,' he said softly. 'I wish I had the chance to change things.'

Anahera's smile was wistful. 'What's that saying? If wishes were horses, then beggars would ride...'

'I've gone over and over it, you know. Wondering

why I *didn't* tell you—or anyone else—about Jane. I think it was because I was…escaping, you know?'

Luke had the most beautiful face Anahera had ever seen on a man. She loved the intensity of his eyes. The way he could control his face when he was in a professional setting but he could let it go sometimes, like now, when every emotion could be seen in the subtle dance of muscle movement. It was how she knew how open he was being. How honest.

'Those years with Jane in the coma. Being married but having no wife… It was the loneliest place you could imagine. And I was trapped in it. As trapped as Jane was in her own body. It never occurred to me that I'd want to be with anyone else, though, because when I was in London I knew she was lying in a bed in the same city and it would have felt like cheating.' He closed his eyes for a moment. 'It *would* have been cheating.'

Had Jane known how much she had been loved? How many men were capable of such loyalty and devotion?

'Coming here—to Wildfire Island—was a crazy idea that my boss came up with because he said if I didn't take a break, he'd either have to fire me or I'd kill myself by overworking.'

A smile tugged one corner of his mouth. 'And coming here was like being set free from that trap. London was a world away. I couldn't visit Jane. There was nothing here to even remind me. It was a fantasy break and I had been given permission to forget—just for a few weeks. I guess telling anyone would have broken that fantasy.'

Anahera's head dipped in a slow nod. She could understand that.

'I hadn't expected to meet you, though. To…to fall in love…'

The words seemed to explode in her head. Luke *had* loved her. He still did, if the expression in his eyes were anything to go by. And then he touched her face again, and she had to close her eyes. Tightly, but that wasn't enough to prevent a tear escaping.

'I know I hurt you.' Luke's voice was raw now. 'And if I could change anything by turning back time, that would be the one thing I would change. But by the time I did try to put things right it was too late, wasn't it? And I'd been in a bad space when I called you anyway. It was just after the funeral. I didn't expect to be forgiven and I was right so I let it go and never tried again. And you'd already moved on to a new life. You'd found Hana's father…'

Another tear escaped. This was it—the moment of truth. But how could she destroy the love she'd seen in Luke's eyes and inflict more pain on someone who'd already been through too much? Or wipe out the blissful reminder of what it was like to be made love to by someone who thought about her that way?

'Would it have made a difference, Ana? If you'd known about Jane right from the start? Would you have let me close if you'd known I still had a wife?' His sigh was heavy. 'There's another saying—that timing is everything. If only I'd waited a few months before taking that break…'

In the silence that followed his words Anahera made her decision. Maybe it would have been a different one if he hadn't given her such an opportunity but there it was—a perfect lead in to what she'd seen as a framework to cling to.

'It was a fantasy, Luke.' Her voice sounded almost rusty and she had to clear her throat gently. 'For me as much as you, I think. History trying to repeat itself, I think.'

'You've said that before. About raising Hana by yourself.' Luke was frowning. 'I'm not sure I understand what you mean now, though.'

'I mean that I knew it couldn't have worked. I only have to remember my mother crying over photographs of my father to know that.'

She felt the touch of Luke's hand as he stroked her hair. 'I remember you saying that he'd died when you were very young. That was a tragedy.' Luke's smile was crooked. 'But I'm not planning on dying any time, soon, Ana.'

'That's not what I meant. The real tragedy was that they loved each other so much but couldn't find a way to be together all the time because they came from such different worlds. And he died in France. Mum couldn't afford for us to go to his funeral even, and his family wouldn't pay. They thought he'd been crazy, marrying a girl from a Pacific island who didn't want to live in Paris.' Anahera could see that Luke was processing what she was saying. Was he relating the story to himself? Wondering if she had no desire to live in London?

'She tried,' Anahera added. 'She took me to Paris when I was a baby and we lived there for a few months. She said that, despite being so in love with my father, it was the loneliest time and that she couldn't live without the sun. And he couldn't live full time in a place that was a holiday destination for him. It had just been a fantasy…'

Luke's face had stilled. Whatever emotion he was feeling was hidden. 'So you're saying you wouldn't consider trying something like that? Living in a different place? Did you hate being in Brisbane that much?'

Given different circumstances, Anahera would have loved Brisbane, with the vibrancy of a big city and new things to entertain and challenge her. But she couldn't tell Luke that because it would undermine the integrity of her framework.

'I needed to come home,' she whispered. 'I needed my family.'

Luke nodded. 'I think I understand,' he said slowly.

His hand was on her shoulder now. He traced the length of her arm until he found her fingers and he raised her hand to place a kiss on her palm.

'You were in love with me, too, weren't you, Ana? Or did I imagine that?'

'You didn't imagine it.' Her voice cracked but she carried on. 'I loved you more than I thought it was possible to love anyone. I…' She had to bite her lip so that she didn't tell him she still felt exactly the same way.

'And I felt exactly the same way about you,' Luke murmured. 'We never really got round to telling each other that properly, did we?'

'No.'

'And it's too late now.'

Anahera's heart was breaking. But this wasn't just about her, was it? She had to remember that and hold on to it.

'It was always too late, Luke. We just didn't know it.'

In response, Luke drew her into his arms and held

her close. She could feel his heart beating against her own. An echo of his voice rumbling in his chest.

'If this *is* just a fantasy...would there be any reason for us not to enjoy it for a bit longer? Just a few days more?'

He was kissing her hair now. Stroking her back. Their lovemaking had been so wild and fierce as they'd slaked their pent-up need for each other. What would it be like to do it again—the way they used to make love, with that slow tenderness that took its own sweet time to build to such a passionate release?

'How soon do you need to be home?'

With a sigh, Anahera let go of rational thought and lifted her face as she pulled Luke's head close enough for her to touch his lips with her own.

'Not for a while,' she murmured. 'Long enough...'

CHAPTER SEVEN

SOMETHING WEIRD HAD happened today.

Perhaps it was some kind of emotional alchemy from a mix of grief, desire and that bone-deep contentment that only came in the wake of complete physical fulfilment.

If someone had asked, Anahera would have said with absolute conviction that it wasn't possible to love Hana more than she already did.

And yet here she was, looking down at her sleeping daughter, filled with love that had a new depth, and it was overwhelming enough to make her heart ache and for slow tears to trace the outline of her nose.

Was it because she'd been part of the grief of Tane's family as they'd faced the loss of someone so deeply loved?

It couldn't be that simple. It wasn't the first time she'd lost a patient, and while every death saddened her it was a part of the job she had chosen to do and one that was as much a part of her as being a mother. Even the really tragic cases like Tane and little Hami—the child they'd lost to the same, awful disease of encephalitis a couple of years ago—could be processed in a way that made her a better nurse.

A better person even, because they served to remind her how precious life was and how important it was to show the people in her life how much they were loved.

This new level of love for Hana felt like she had tapped into a mysterious vault where there was a vast new wealth of love to be found—and shared.

Could it be because she felt loved herself in a way that nobody but Luke could have made her feel?

The soft mosquito netting slipped through her fingers as Anahera stepped back from the bed after a final kiss and murmurs of love, but her train of thought was not interrupted.

Was love like some kind of emotional currency and the more you could put into the bank, the more you had to draw on?

The smile of greeting from Vailea as she went onto the veranda almost started her tears again. How could anyone get so much understanding and sympathy into one smile?

'You've had such a day, love. Come and sit. Eat. I've made the paella you love.'

Anahera glanced at her favourite chair that she couldn't wait to sink into and at the plate of fragrant rice and seafood—one of Vailea's specialties—that was waiting on the little round table beside the chair. She took a step farther away first, though, so that she could press her cheek to her mother's hair for a long moment.

'Thanks, Mum. Love you.'

'And I love you. Now sit. Eat.'

Anahera sat. And ate. And smiled.

She had all the love she needed in her life, didn't she? From Hana and her mother. From her friends like Sam and Hettie and Keanu and Caroline. From the island community that was more like a huge, extended family that willingly shared the joy of celebrations and was there as a solid rock of support when things weren't so good.

But the love that Luke could give her was different, her mind whispered.

Important…

Her mother sat there quietly, keeping her company as she ate her meal. Every so often she would glance at Anahera, who smiled back but said nothing. She needed this comfort. The delicious food, the company of someone so dear and the peacefulness of home that wrapped around her like a cosmic hug.

It was Vailea who broke the silence.

'I was worried about you,' she said. 'I knew you'd gone walking because you were so upset about Tane and I thought you still would be when you came home but…' Her glance was quizzical. 'There's something different about you.'

The last mouthful of her food was a little difficult to swallow. Just how much could her mother see?

'I'm just the same, Mum. I am still upset about Tane—of course I am—but I feel better than I did. The sunset was beautiful. I…guess I found some peace on the beach…'

'Mmm…' It was obvious that Vailea knew she was being fobbed off. She wouldn't push for more of an explanation and maybe that was partly why Anahera felt she deserved more.

'I met Luke,' she added. 'And we talked. He was even more upset than I was, I think. He took losing Tane as a personal failure. He told Sam there was nothing more he could do here and that he was going to go back to London tomorrow.'

'But what about all that research? Didn't he want to go and collect tea-leaves and things?'

'I think he's changed his mind and he's going to stay for a bit longer. He was angry with himself, I think. Like it was his fault Tane died.'

'That's ridiculous. I've never seen a doctor work so hard to save someone. Or care so much. He's an extraordinary young man.' She sighed. 'You know, when he was here the first time I had hopes that something might happen between the two of you. He's just the sort of man I could see you with. I hear he's good with children, too. Marama has been helping me in the kitchen and she was telling me all about the football game over on French Island.' She shook her head. 'It was such a shock to find out he was married.'

'His wife died just after he went back. It's a really sad story. She'd had a dreadful accident and was in a coma for years. The only time she opened her eyes and spoke was when he was here. That's why he rushed back like that.'

'Ohhh...'

Anahera could almost hear the wheels turning in her mother's brain.

'Even if I was looking for a partner—which I'm not—I wouldn't choose someone who lives half a world away. I know how that works.' Her smile was poignant. 'I saw you crying too often when I was little.'

Vailea's eyes widened. 'But that was because Stefan *died*. I lost the father of my baby and the man I loved with all my heart...'

An echo of Luke's voice was as clear as if he was whispering in her ear.

I'm not planning on dying any time, soon, Ana.

'But you couldn't live together. He came from Paris and you said it was cold and horrible and you couldn't live without the sun.'

'I didn't want to live without Stefan either.' Her mother's voice was quiet. Sad. 'We would have found a way to make it work. Paris in the summer is probably wonderful, and who wouldn't have wanted to escape a European winter by living in a tropical paradise? We were working it out. We *would* have worked it out but he…he died.'

'Oh, Mum…' Anahera reached over the little table to hold and squeeze her mother's hand. She could hear the tears in Vailea's voice, and the old grief was contagious. It didn't matter how much love she or Hana or anyone else could give, did it? There was still that gap that could never be filled.

And maybe she needed the comfort of touch herself. The conviction in her mother's voice had shocked her because they had knocked the bolts from the framework of the rationale she'd been using as the justification to keep the truth from Luke and maintain the foundations of the future unchanged. Her mother truly believed it would have been possible to live in different worlds and to be with the man she loved so much. To have a whole family.

The bolts were gone. It would take no more than a puff of breath to topple the emotional structure completely, and then where would she be?

Nursing even more guilt than ever before, that was where.

'He wasn't going to let you grow up without a daddy. He adored you. And me…' Vailea sniffed and sighed again. 'There's never been anyone else for me. I doubt there ever will be.'

'I'm...sorry...'

Inadequate words but the sorrow Anahera was feeling was genuine. For her mother, but for herself, too. She couldn't remember her father so she couldn't miss *him* but she had always been aware of that gap in her life so she had always missed having him in her life. Having a father like the other kids had.

It was in that moment that she knew what she had to do.

It was wrong to keep the truth from Luke. She had to tell him. She had to tell Hana, too. She wasn't just depriving Luke of a daughter. She was depriving Hana of a father. If her daughter ever found out the truth, she would never forgive her mother.

Anahera would never forgive herself.

She would also have to tell her mother—something she should have done right from the start.

Maybe that would be the easiest way to start. Anahera took a very deep breath as she tried to collect the words she needed.

'Mum?'

'Yes, love?'

'There's something I need to tell you.'

'What's that?' Vailea was distracted, fishing in the pocket of her apron. 'I'm sure I've got a hanky in here somewhere...'

Her sniff revealed that she was still crying. How could Anahera make things worse by dropping the bombshell hovering on her lips right now?

And, if she told her mother, it was only a step away from telling Luke and that was...

It was terrifying.

Even if she started by telling him that there was a chance they could work things out and be together, she would have to destroy whatever hope that engendered by telling him the truth about Hana and then she would be back to square one. He would hate her for lying to him and he might demand a share of Hana's life but exclude her from the time he had with his daughter and everything she had feared the most would come to pass.

She had dug a huge hole for herself and there was no way out. She couldn't even see the frayed ends of a rope.

Vailea had found her handkerchief and she blew her nose. Then she patted Anahera's hand and smiled, signalling that she had pulled herself together and things were going to be fine again.

'Look at me...sitting here crying when I have so much I can be thankful for. When other people have so much more to try and bear. Poor Tane. And that poor little baby, who's going to grow up without a daddy. Like you did...' She shook her head. 'What was it that you wanted to tell me, love?'

Her words felt like a judgement and as if she was the guilty party. Confessing had suddenly become so much harder. So much scarier.

Anahera swallowed hard. 'Just...that I love you.'

She didn't dare meet her mother's eyes because she knew that too much would be seen. In the heartbeat of silence following her words, she knew that avoiding that contact hadn't been enough.

Vailea might not know what was wrong but she certainly knew that that there was something she wasn't being told.

'I love you, too, Anahera.'

Her heart sank. Her full name was only ever used when things were serious.

'And you know that my ears are here for whenever you want to talk about anything.'

'I know,' Anahera whispered. 'I…I can't, Mum. Not yet. There's…um…someone else I probably need to talk to first.'

This silence was broken by the creak of the old wicker chair as Vailea got to her feet. By the clink of cutlery against china as she picked up Anahera's plate.

'It's hard to do the right thing sometimes,' Vailea said quietly. 'But, in the end, sometimes the right thing is the only thing you *can* do.'

Anahera nodded.

She knew that.

She just had to find the courage she needed to do it.

Of all his five senses, Luke decided that the one he would least like to lose might be that of smell.

It hit him even before he opened his eyes as the first fingers of light poked their way through the slats of the shutters the next morning.

That had been the thing that had hit him like a brick the moment he'd set foot on this island again, hadn't it? That gentle, tropical breeze with the sweet waft of flowers like frangipani and jasmine.

For him, it would also remind him of the scent of Anahera's hair. Of her skin.

He kept his eyes shut as he took a deep breath, his nose still half buried in the soft pillow.

Her scent was still on his sheets, but even if it hadn't been, it was so deeply embedded in his memory that it would be an instant connection for the rest of his life. Interesting how closely it was related to the sense of taste because that was what filled his mind now as he surfaced to complete consciousness.

The taste of Ana...

Good grief...and how close were they both to the sense of touch? The memories were so recent and real it felt like he could roll over and start making love to her again this very second, and the desire to do exactly that was so powerful he threw back the covers with a groan and pushed his body to get his feet on the floor and start moving.

Towards the shower. Preferably a cold one.

Or maybe a swim would be more effective. Grabbing a towel and a dry pair of swimming shorts, Luke headed out into the soft light of dawn and jogged along the track to the beach. He dropped the towel without pausing and kept running until the water was deep enough to slow his momentum and then he dived and started kicking. By the time he surfaced and could use his arms, he was swimming as hard and fast as he had been yesterday, in an attempt to wash tension from his body and calm the kaleidoscope of thoughts and emotions in his head.

When he started to tire, he rolled onto his back and floated on gentle undulations of the deep water and watched the sun climb over the ragged mountaintops.

He never saw the sun rise in London. Rarely noticed a sunset either. And he never, ever went swimming because he could only do that in a pool and the smell of chlorine was one he associated with grief because that had been the scent of Jane's skin when he'd arrived at the emergency department that dreadful day.

This was, indeed, a very different world.

A fantasy?

But it felt real. He could feel the water around his body and he could see the clear blue of the lightening sky that heralded another perfect day. If he turned his head he could see the curve of that gorgeous beach with the twisted shapes of the old fig trees near the bottom of the cliffs, and if he let his mind wander just the tiniest bit he could see Anahera standing on the sand, waiting for him.

The image was real enough to start him swimming towards the shore, but as he stood up and shook the sea water from his eyes he could see that he was alone on Sunset Beach.

Of course the image had been a fantasy. Anahera would be at home with her family, caring for her daughter and getting ready for work. Getting on with a life that was so far removed from his own life that her words came back to haunt him.

'The real tragedy was that they loved each other so much but couldn't find a way to be together all the time because they came from such different worlds...

'I needed to come home...I needed my family...'

She'd been right. It was a fantasy because it was too much to believe that real life could deliver this kind of paradise.

It wasn't the setting. Luke draped his towel over

his shoulders and took in a last glance of the dramatic beauty around him before making his way slowly back to the bure and the luxury of the shower. Everyone could visit this kind of tropical paradise that travel agents loved to advertise with huge posters in their windows to lure in Londoners in the grey depths of winter.

That it was paradise for him had nothing to do with being on a remote island.

It had everything to do with being with Ana.

And she belonged here. She needed to be here. How could he even think of taking her away from the sun? To a place where the scent of flowers might fade from her hair and her skin and that light in her eyes that was like a personal sun might begin to dim?

Would it make it all the harder to go home if they made the most of the few days they could have together now?

As if he had a choice...

A wry smile curled Luke's lips as he flicked the shower on and reached for the soap that had yet another scented reminder of Ana to release.

It didn't really matter if it made things harder. They were going to be unbearable for a while anyway.

'So that's it.' Sam spread the pages he had just collected from the printer on the staffroom table in front of where Luke was sitting. 'The whole plan for the rollout of the clinical trial. We've covered every island and hopefully we'll get a good cross-section of the population to sign up.' He grinned at Luke. 'Not a bad day's work, is it? Could I interest you in a beer?'

'Sounds good.' The glance Luke sent in Anahera's

direction was hopefully casual. 'You going to have one, Ana?'

'Why not?' Anahera opened the fridge and took out some cans. 'It's been the longest day. Too quiet...'

They only had a couple of inpatients and there'd been no dramas. Nothing to push the awareness of that empty bed in the intensive care room to the background. Nothing to break the sad silence that seemed to echo in the corridors and wards. It would be nice to sit here for a few minutes and celebrate something as positive as the start of a trial that could prevent future tragedies from fatal cases of encephalitis.

'We still need to map out the epidemiological study that you want me to do.' Sam popped the tab on his can and took a gulp of the cold beer. 'And what about the tea-leaves stuff? Do you want to leave that to me, too? Or there's always Keanu... Hey...' Sam grinned at Anahera. 'I forgot to tell you that Keanu's coming back next week.'

'Is he? Is Caroline coming with him?'

'Are you kidding? As if they'd let each other out of their sights right now...'

She couldn't help catching Luke's glance as she smiled. She knew how that felt—not wanting to let someone out of your sight. And then her smile faded as she hurriedly looked away. It hadn't just been the empty bed she'd been so conscious of all day. Knowing that Luke was in the hospital, working with Sam, had been in her mind just as much. The day had been so long because she'd been counting the minutes until they might be able to have some time alone together.

Time that she would have to use to tell him the truth.

Anahera stared at the can of beer she was holding so tightly the chill from the metal was seeping into her hand. It was time that would spell the end of life as she knew it but her mother had hit the nail on the head. Sometimes you simply didn't have a choice and the only thing to do was the right thing.

It took a moment to tune into what Sam was saying to Luke.

'So it was Keanu's father who started the first research into the tea but it all stopped when he died.'

'What happened to him?'

'Got killed in a rock fall, apparently. Keanu was just a toddler but he's grown up knowing how special his dad was. There's a big picture of him in his graduation gown in the entrance to Atangi School. He was their brightest star back then, and the Lockhart family funded him to go to the mainland to get his degree.' Sam nodded with satisfaction. 'I reckon Keanu would see the project as a way of honouring his dad's memory. He'd love to be involved.'

'I'd still like to see where the bushes grow and take some photos. I'd like to take some leaves back to London, too, and get the experts to analyse them to see what makes them different.'

'I could help you collect them. I know where the bushes grow.' Anahera's brain was buzzing. French Island was the place they'd really started talking to each other. It would be the ideal place to have an even more significant conversation, wouldn't it—except that would mean having to wait. 'We couldn't do it tomorrow because it's Tane's funeral but the day after that, we could visit the island.' She was speaking fast because this felt like a plan coming together. The first step in putting things right. 'We'd have to take a boat, though. We couldn't justify a helicopter when there isn't a clinic happening.'

'Make a day of it,' Sam suggested. 'Take a picnic. Take Hana with you. Hey…take Bugsy with you. He loves a boat ride.'

Luke found himself smiling as he listened to the conversation. It sounded like a great idea. How amazing would it be to be out with Anahera and her gorgeous little girl, with a dog bounding along beside them?

Like the perfect picture of a family outing…

Another image for the fantasy gallery he'd be able to treasure for the rest of his life?

Anahera didn't seem so keen on the idea, though. Weirdly, she was looking…nervous?

Sam was still on a roll. 'Speaking of Hana, don't forget she's due for her vaccination.'

'What?' Anahera's eyes widened. 'You want to start the encephalitis trial with *Hana*?'

'I'm talking about her four-year vaccination. The one for diphtheria, tetanus, whooping cough and polio. And the MMR, if she didn't have it at eighteen months.'

The colour had suddenly drained from Anahera's face, and Luke stared at her in astonishment. Was it that big a deal for her to take her daughter to an appointment that involved a painful injection? She was a nurse, for heaven's sake—she knew how important vaccinations were.

Sam was taking another pull of his beer and didn't seem to notice her odd reaction. 'Did she have the MMR at eighteen months? You were still in Brisbane then, weren't you?'

'I'll find the records for you. She's not due for ages yet.'

'Two weeks isn't ages. I noticed the reminder on my calendar this morning.'

Luke was still staring at Anahera and barely listening to Sam. It wasn't just her face that was pale. Her hand was squeezing that can so hard her fingers looked white. Any harder and…yes…the can crumpled and a whoosh of foamy liquid spilled over her hand and onto the table.

'Oops…' Sam scooped paper out of harm's way.

Anahera leapt up to grab a tea towel.

Luke was aware of an odd buzzing in his head like static as his brain finally caught up with what Sam had said. He didn't stop to think before saying something. He wasn't actually aware he was saying it aloud.

'Hana's only three and a half.'

'No…' Sam was tapping the sheaf of paper in his hand on the table top to straighten the edges. 'She turns four in a couple of weeks. Vailea's already talking about the cake she's going to make, isn't she, Ana?'

For the longest moment the only sound in the room was the last edge of the papers being tapped.

The moment was more than long enough for Luke's brain to focus on a few simple calculations.

Calculations that lead to a blindingly clear result.

Anahera had lied to him.

Hana was six months older than he'd been led to

believe. Anahera hadn't hooked up with someone as soon as she had moved to Brisbane. She'd already been pregnant when she'd left Wildfire Island.

Hana had to be *his* daughter...

CHAPTER EIGHT

'ANA? ARE YOU OKAY?'

It was the concern in Sam's voice that made Anahera realise that she was frozen to the spot, the tea towel dangling from her hands while the foamy puddle on the table spread out and started dripping from the edge. She looked up slowly but her gaze didn't connect to Sam's. It was drawn, inexorably, to Luke.

The shock on his face was only to be expected but the darkness behind it was far more disturbing. Anger? No, it was worse than that. It looked more like...devastation.

In her peripheral vision she could see Sam's head turning to look at Luke, too, and even someone who had only a fraction of his intelligence and compassion would have realised that something major was happening between Anahera and Luke.

'I...ah...I'd better go and file these papers so I don't lose them.' Sam took a step towards the door but then hesitated, and this time Anahera looked at her friend directly because she knew what he was thinking. She was in trouble and he would do whatever she wanted him to do to help.

The almost imperceptible shake of her head told

him that she didn't need him to stay. That this was something she had to deal with by herself.

She was still staring at the door after he left, too afraid to look back at Luke, so his quiet words made her jump.

'I'm right, aren't I? Hana is my daughter.'

'Yes.' Her response was no more than a whisper.

'Were you going to tell me?' His voice was cold now. So cold that Anahera felt a shiver trickle down her spine.

'*Yes...*' She gulped in some air. 'Today. But...but then...then I thought that if we were going to go to French Island together that would be a better time but...' The words were tumbling out with desperate haste. 'But you liked Sam's idea of a picnic and taking Hana and that wouldn't have been...' Her voice cracked, and Anahera knew that she wasn't going to be able to hold her tears at bay.

The urge to throw herself into Luke's arms so that he could hold her while she sobbed out the overwhelming mix of guilt and apology and...yes...*relief* was so strong she could feel her body leaning into the movement.

'I don't believe you.'

The words—and the tone—were a brick wall that Anahera slammed against. Her balance had tipped enough for her to need to catch the back of a chair and the support was comforting enough to make her slip into the seat.

'You lied to me, Ana.'

There was a note of outrage in his voice. Disappointment that was so personal it was a direct body blow. She'd been right to fear that he would hate her for what she'd done.

'*No...*' It wasn't that she was trying to contradict him—more like she was trying to ward off what she knew had to be coming next—but her response drew a huff of disbelief from Luke.

'*No?*' A chair scraped as Luke pulled it out and dropped himself into it. The tension in his body seemed to be transferred through the tabletop like the faint aftershock of an earthquake. 'Oh...right. You told me the truth, didn't you? That Hana was born in Brisbane. That her father was a doctor. That—what was it you said exactly? That her father wasn't in the picture because there'd never been any chance of a relationship with him?'

'I didn't think there was. I thought you were married. Living in London. I didn't *know...*'

'And whose fault was that, Ana?'

'Mine.' She had to hide her tears so she put her elbows on the table and covered her face with her hands. '*Mine...*'

'And the only relationship you thought to consider was one you might have yourself? Did it not even occur to you that I might have had the right to have a relationship with my own child? My *daughter*?'

The sound that escaped Luke now was—horrifyingly—close to a sob. And then he was completely silent, as though the enormity of what he'd just found out was only now sinking in.

The silence went on. And on. But all Anahera could do was wait. To wallow in the revelation of how selfish she'd been.

How wrong...

* * *

He had a daughter.

Something was swimming through the shock of the discovery and the disbelief that he hadn't been told. A feeling Luke couldn't identify clearly because he'd never experienced it before.

Maybe it was a very personal kind of amazement. He had a daughter. A small person who carried his genes. Who was a part of himself. A child who was about to reach the milestone of being alive for four years and he knew nothing about her, except that she was beautiful.

And she loved butterflies.

And he could have gone back to London and carried on with the rest of his life and never known that she even existed.

'How could you do that?' The words burst out and he wasn't surprised that they made Anahera flinch.

The pang of disappointment in himself that he'd scared her might well come back later to haunt him, but in this moment he didn't care.

'When you knew the truth, you still didn't tell me. How could you have been with me last night…?' The memory of how it had felt to hold her in his arms—to make love to her—was trying to swamp him. Like a drowning man, he had to kick hard to reach the surface.

'It was all a lie, wasn't it? You can't tell someone you loved them more than you thought it was possible to love anyone but…but know that you're doing something like *this* to them…' He stared at Anahera's bent head, willing her to look up and meet his gaze.

'I thought I knew you,' he said sadly. 'But I don't,

do I? And you know what?' The scraping of his chair on the floor was as harsh as his tone as he stood up. 'I don't think I want to any more.'

The need for distance was imperative—before he said something he knew he would regret. Something cruel that would make her feel a fraction of the pain he was feeling right now.

But he hesitated for a heartbeat.

'Why, Ana?' He closed his eyes on a sigh. 'Just tell me why. The real reason, not that cop-out about history repeating itself. Why didn't you tell me when you had the chance? When we were sitting on that cliff and I asked…I *asked* about Hana's father? When I said…' His breath came out in an incredulous huff as he opened his eyes again. 'When I said he must have been over the moon to have a daughter like Hana. You could have just said that he didn't know he had a daughter and I would have put two and two together.'

Luke ran stiff fingers through his hair and ended up holding his head as if there was too much inside and it might explode.

'Why?'

Finally, Anahera raised her face and looked directly at him. Her eyes were so dark they looked like bottomless pools. And they were so full of fear Luke felt the hairs on the back of his neck stand up.

Her voice was so strangled it sounded nothing like her. 'I thought you might take her away from me.'

Unbelievably, there was a new pain to be experienced. One that held the threat of a chasm he really, really didn't want to see into.

'I loved you, Ana.' It was even painful to try and

swallow. 'How could you believe that I would have done something to hurt you?'

Loved.

Past tense.

It was no more than she had expected, but she hadn't expected it to hurt *this* much.

Anahera watched Luke walk out the door of the staffroom and knew that she hadn't ever really known what loneliness felt like until now.

Luke's parting words had been a mutter about needing space. Or time to think. She'd barely heard them because the implications of that choice of tense had been crowding into her head with the singsong kind of 'I told you so' taunt. And her heart had been dealing with the sensation of the distance between them increasing as he'd moved towards the door. Of a bond being pulled beyond capacity and snapping with a vicious whip-like crack that was leaving blood to well in its wake.

The worst had happened.

Or had it? Maybe there was worse to come. Maybe Luke wouldn't have tried to take her daughter away from her when he'd loved her but now he didn't know who she was and he didn't even *want* to know so there was no chance he would ever love her again, which meant that there was no barrier to him doing something that might hurt her. When he'd had time to think, would he decide that it might be a good idea to take Hana away from someone who treated the people she loved the way she had treated him?

Oh… God…

Telling the truth was supposed to lessen guilt,

wasn't it? So why was it worse? The need to protect her family and her life by keeping the truth hidden had outweighed the guilt until now, but now that side of the scales had been replaced by fear and it seemed in perfect balance with the guilt on the other side.

Whatever was going to happen, she had brought it on herself.

But that didn't mean she couldn't still fight to protect her mother and Hana and herself, did it?

Her hands were steepled on either side of her nose. Moving them apart, she scraped away the tears beneath her eyes as she took in a deep breath that sounded like a final sniff. Sitting here, crying, wasn't going to help anyone.

Luke wouldn't be sitting around anywhere. He was probably swimming by now. Powering through the ocean as he cleared his head and decided what he was going to do next.

Or had he gone to find his daughter?

The thought was appalling. What if Luke told Hana who he was before Anahera had had time to prepare her for something that would be confusing and probably frightening?

It was enough to propel her from her chair and through the door. It was only luck that stopped her barrelling straight into her mother.

Vailea rarely left her domain of the hospital kitchens to come into the staffroom and, by the look on her face, she hadn't come to check the supplies of cold drinks in the staff fridge.

'So Sam was right...' Vailea shook her head. 'Oh, love...'

'Sam doesn't know...' Anahera stepped back. She

could see the fear in her mother's eyes. She *knew*...
Did everybody know now? 'What did he say?'

'Just that you seemed to be upset about something.
That Luke was, too. And it had been something he'd
said about Hana that had caused it. About how old she
was...' Her breath came out in a sigh. 'It wasn't hard
for him to guess, love, and...and I've always had my
suspicions.'

'You never said.'

'I thought he was married. I thought...last night
that you'd decided to tell the truth and it seemed like
the right thing to do was to tell him first.'

'I didn't get the chance. And now he doesn't believe
that I was ever going to.'

'Well, I can tell him *that* isn't true.'

Anahera shook her head. 'It wouldn't make any
difference. Not now. I should have told him before...
before...' Tears threatened again. Before she'd made
things worse by deliberately *not* telling him? Before
she'd given in to the temptation of making love with
him again?

'He's not even here now. I don't know where he is
and I'm scared he might have gone off to find Hana...'
The need to get to Hana first came back with renewed
strength, and Anahera started to move but Vailea
caught her arm.

'Hana's safe. Luke went storming off towards his
bure and Sam's gone after him.'

'Why?'

'To talk to him. To try and help.'

'Talking won't be enough. I need to get legal advice. Maybe Caroline or Keanu could help me find
someone while they're still on the mainland. I'll ring

and talk to them tonight. I'll fix this, Mum. I won't let him take Hana away from us.'

'Oh, darling...why would he want to do that?'

'Because...' The calm tone of reason in her mother's voice was taking the wind out of the sails Anahera had hoisted in readiness for the new fight she might have to protect her family. Her voice dropped to a whisper. 'Because she's his daughter...'

'And I suspect that the only thing he'll want to do right now is to meet her properly. And he has every right to do that, hasn't he?'

'Yes...'

'That's why I told Sam to bring him round to our house later. For dinner.'

'Mum...' Anahera was horrified. Home was her safe place, only secondary to these islands. Having the truth in the open was making her feel vulnerable enough. Having Luke in her home with her daughter—*their* daughter—was a terrifying prospect. Were they going to tell Hana who Luke really was? How? And when?

'It's a start,' Vailea said quietly. 'Remember what I said to you last night? About the only thing to do being the right thing?'

Sometimes her mother could make her feel like a child again. A child who still had a lot to learn. Anahera nodded.

'Well, this is one of those right things. Now, why don't you go and pick up Hana and go home? See if you can find some pretty flowers on the way and she could help you make a bowl for the table. I want to go down to the boats and get some nice fresh fish.'

'He won't come. He doesn't want to see me at the

moment.' Her voice dropped. 'He…he hates me, Mum. Because I lied to him.'

'He doesn't hate you.' Vailea touched her daughter's cheek gently, and the expression in her eyes made Anahera want to cry.

'If he hated you, how could you both have made something as perfect as our little Hana?'

'That was then. It's different now.'

'True love never dies. He's angry right now and he has every right to be like that. He's probably confused, too. It changes you, being a parent. You had nine months to get used to the idea. Imagine if someone just handed you a baby and told you that you were a mother now. How would you feel?'

'Terrified,' Anahera admitted. 'I wouldn't have the first idea what to do.'

'Exactly. And how much harder would it be if the baby was big enough to have her own opinions and tell you what they were?'

Being terrified was not something she would ever have thought Luke would have to contend with but her mother's words were making sense. Whatever emotions Luke was experiencing had to be strong enough to need an outlet, and anger was usually the fastest route to ease the initial pressure, wasn't it?

It had been for her.

That apparent betrayal in finding out that Luke was married had made her angry enough to slam the door on his attempt to see her again and put things right. She had convinced herself that the last thing she ever wanted was to see him again.

Luke couldn't slam that kind of door because Hana would be left on the other side and however difficult it might be for him to face the woman who'd betrayed *him*, Anahera knew instinctively that Luke would never contemplate turning his back on his own daughter.

Neutral ground would have to be found. If nothing else, maybe they could end up with a kind of friendship and that would be better than nothing, wouldn't it?

Vailea looked over her shoulder as she turned to leave. 'Let's make Luke welcome in our home, love. He's part of our family. And we have something to thank him for, don't we?'

Anahera was still trying to answer the question she had just posed for herself. 'Do we?'

'Think about it.' With a smile, her mother was gone.

But Anahera's thoughts were still on her question about whether friendship would be better than nothing and she'd found her answer by the time she headed out into the heat of the late afternoon to collect Hana from the Lockhart mansion.

No. It definitely wouldn't.

Friendship with Luke would be a minefield of memories that would taunt her with 'what might have been' and it would reinforce the level of where a bar had been set and she would never meet anyone else who could possibly match that level.

But what could she do?

If she fostered a less-than-amicable relationship with her child's father, she would be bringing nuances of hostility into the life of a little girl who had never known—or shown—anything other than love.

The smile on Hana's face when she saw her mother was more than enough to convince Anahera that she couldn't do something that would affect her daughter's happiness. Especially something that would prick the happy bubble she lived in right now, where everybody loved each other and nothing could threaten that ultimate security. The tight hug she received from those tiny arms was enough to remind her how incredibly lucky she was to have this small person in her life.

And that was when the penny dropped.

This unimaginable joy that loving and being loved by Hana bestowed was what Luke deserved thanks for.

Without him, Hana would not have existed.

CHAPTER NINE

LUKE HAD FACED life-changing moments before.

Like the moment his pager had sounded as he had been preparing for an early-morning ward round to relay the message that his wife was being rushed to the emergency department of his own hospital, under CPR.

He'd known that his life was never going to be the same and he would never forget the way he'd felt as he'd run through those corridors, dodging people and beds and trollies—barely seeing what had been around him as he'd run headlong into an unknown and frightening future. That feeling of fighting against a force that had the potential to suffocate him. A force that could make it impossible to breathe and make his whole world grow dark. A force that he had no ability to control.

Even if he hadn't been able to remember it so well, it would have come flooding back right now, as he walked towards the village beside Sam and Bugsy. How, exactly, had Sam persuaded him to come here?

'You need a bridge,' he'd said, *'to get past the gap that's just appeared in the ground in front of you. It's much, much harder to build a bridge like that by*

yourself. When you've got other people around you, they can help find what you need to build it with. Besides, it's about time you met your daughter properly, isn't it?'

Maybe the beer had helped, when Sam had taken him to the conference centre's bar. And maybe it was the reminder that this was the exact spot he'd first seen Anahera again had been why he'd had another one.

Whatever. He was here now, silently walking up the garden path that led to the village house where the Kopu family lived.

His daughter was inside that house.

Or maybe not. A tiny figure was crouched beside a bushy, flower-laden shrub and she hadn't noticed the new arrivals until Bugsy sat beside her, his feathered tail waving vigorously enough to tickle a small brown bare leg.

'No, Bugsy! You can't eat it.' Hana's head turned and there was a worried frown above those huge, dark eyes that Luke remembered from the one time he'd seen her. 'Make him go 'way, Uncle Sam.'

'What's up, chicken?'

Stepping away from Luke, Sam crouched down beside Hana with an ease that gave Luke a pang of something that felt like jealousy. Sam already had a relationship with Hana—clearly one they were both very comfortable with.

'Oh, I see… It's a caterpillar.'

Hana nodded her head. 'A patercillar. And Bugsy wants to eat it and if he does, it won't turn into a flutterby.'

It brought a smile to Luke's lips, the adorable way Hana jumbled her words, but the smile wobbled and he realised—with horror—that he was on the verge of tears.

'Bugsy won't eat it,' Sam was saying reassuringly. 'He knows that caterpillars don't taste nice. And he thinks he's a person, not a bird or a gecko. He wants some of that yummy food that your nana is cooking for us.'

Hana heaved a relieved sigh and scrambled up to throw her arms around the dog's neck.

'I love you, Bugsy.'

The prickle of tears was more insistent. Luke cleared his throat to regain control, and the sound made Sam glance up.

'Hey, Hana. This is Luke. He's a friend of mine and Mummy's.'

Her cheek was pressed against Bugsy's golden coat but two eyes swivelled to look directly up at him. He could sense the shyness. The space, hanging in time, that would eventually lead to a decision about whether or not he would be granted entry into her special world.

That space felt like an impassable distance.

'Luke comes from London,' Sam continued. 'That's a country a long, long way away over the sea. Do you reckon they've got butterflies in London?'

'No-o-o...' Hana giggled and peeped up at Luke again.

He smiled. 'We do,' he told her. 'In a place called the London Zoo there's a special house that got built to look like a big caterpillar and inside there are hundreds and hundreds of butterflies.'

Had Sam provided the perfect foundation for a

bridge to span that daunting space? It certainly felt increasingly easy to talk to this little girl.

'Big ones and tiny ones,' he continued. 'All different colours, like black and white and orange and red and yellow.'

Hana's eyes widened. Sam was grinning.

'How would you know that, Luke? Don't tell me you're a butterfly fanatic, too.'

'I do love butterflies,' Luke admitted. 'Always have. I've got a big book about them that I got given for my birthday when I was about Hana's age.'

'Are there blue ones?' It was the first time Hana had spoken directly to Luke. 'Blue ones are the bestest.'

'There are loads of blue ones.' Luke's smile widened. 'They *are* the bestest.'

Sam snorted. 'Let's go inside,' he said. 'Before your skills in the English language deteriorate any further.'

Standing up, Sam extended a hand as if it was an automatic thing to do, and Hana scrambled to her feet and put her hand in his. And then she looked up at Luke and it felt like a completely natural thing to do to extend *his* hand on her other side.

And, dear Lord…the feeling when those tiny fingers curled around his was…indescribable.

Huge…

He couldn't find even a single word of greeting as he reached the steps to the veranda, and Anahera appeared at the door of the house. Not that she was looking at his face. Her gaze was fixed at a lower point. At where his hand was holding Hana's.

Maybe they could all feel the shock wave emanating from Anahera because they all stopped moving at exactly the same time. Even Bugsy, who was happily trailing in their wake.

For a heartbeat they were all frozen. Sam wasn't going to find it easy to suggest any building materials for the bridge that was needed here because they would need to be quite substantial.

The help came from a very unexpected direction.

'Mumma...' Hana's face split into a wide grin. 'Bugsy tried to eat my patercillar and Uncle Luke said he loves flutterbies and he said he lives in a patercillar house.'

'You need to wash your hands, darling.' The words were a little difficult to get out from a suddenly dry mouth. 'It's time for dinner.'

How could Luke have done that? Won her daughter's trust so easily? Had he used the knowledge he'd had of Hana's passion for butterflies to his own advantage?

But... *Uncle* Luke? He certainly hadn't taken any unilateral decision to let Hana know who he really was.

A small percentage of the tension in every cell of her body drained away. Enough to relax her lips to allow a subtle curl to the corners of her mouth.

'A caterpillar house? Really?'

Luke looked embarrassed. 'I was telling her about London Zoo. They have a butterfly house that's shaped like a caterpillar.'

Hana had got as far as the front door. She tugged on her mother's skirt. 'Can we go, Mumma? To the flutterby house?'

Anahera's smile vanished. So the conflict of parents living in worlds apart was beginning already. She couldn't help the tight tone to her voice.

'We'll see. Now scoot—I'm going to check in a minute to see if all the dirt gets washed off those hands.'

Hana's disappearance left a silence that could have been awkward except that Sam started moving up the steps. 'Come on, Bugsy. You stay on the veranda. I'll go and get you a bowl of water.'

The distraction increased as Vailea came to the door, wiping her hands on her apron.

'I can do that. Why don't you all sit out here on the veranda? It's much cooler. I'll bring you boys some beer. One for you, too, Ana?'

'I'll get that.' The excuse to escape for a minute or two and try to get used to what was happening was irresistible. She opened bottles of beer and put them on a tray, along with some glasses. Her mother was filling an old enamel bowl with water at the sink.

'You're doing well,' Vailea said quietly. 'And it'll get easier. I'll feed Hana first and then she can go to bed. I don't imagine Sam and Bugsy will stay late and I'll get out of your way later so you and Luke can talk.'

The prospect was terrifying. Anahera had to make an effort to keep her hands steady so that the rattle of glass wouldn't betray her nervousness as she returned to the veranda.

At least she didn't have to try and start a conversation. Hana had beaten her back to the veranda and she was standing beside the low table, her hands clasped together and her face shining with pride as Luke exclaimed over the bowl with its petal mosaic framed by the turquoise glaze.

'You *made* this? Wow…'

'Mumma helped.' Hana was bouncing from one foot to the other. 'We picked the flowers on the way home. I picked all the yellow ones. And the pink ones.'

'It's an art form you'll find on most Pacific islands.' Vailea was smiling at Bugsy's enthusiastic appreciation of his drink. 'We love our flowers.'

'They're pretty,' Hana told Luke with the solemn tone of imparting great wisdom. 'Like flutterbys.'

'They are indeed.'

Luke was smiling at Hana and Anahera found herself staring intently at his face. She knew that expression. Her heart did a funny double flip thing. This was it, wasn't it? The moment he had fallen in love with his daughter.

Sam and Vailea were smiling, too. As if they thought everything was going according to some plan she wasn't privy to. Nerves kicked in again and she had to break the moment before something even more momentous happened—like someone telling Hana who Luke really was.

'We got most of the flowers from around the lagoon. I couldn't believe how bad the mosquitoes were for that time of day. I've never seen so many.'

'I know.' Vailea clicked her tongue as she sat down and started to pour a drink for herself. 'It's appalling. Nobody's been able to get hold of Ian Lockhart. We're hoping that Caroline can sort out the aerial spraying when she gets back next week.'

'Maybe I'll just sort it out myself,' Sam said quietly. 'We can't afford to wait any longer. People are getting bitten far more than in previous years and it's Russian roulette whether they are infected mosquitoes or not.'

Hana was listening to the adults talking. Was it Anahera's imagination or had she edged closer to where Luke was sitting? She took a deep breath. If she had, it was probably because Bugsy had settled at Sam's feet, on Luke's other side.

'*I* got bitten,' Hana said proudly.

'*What?*' Any need to observe the signals of a developing relationship between Luke and Hana evaporated. '*When*? Why didn't you tell me?'

The happy glow faded from Hana's face. She clearly thought she was in some kind of trouble and she didn't know why. And Luke was frowning. Did he think she was a bad mother because she hadn't noticed?

'Wasn't it itchy?' Luke tilted his head to catch Hana's gaze. 'Did you have to scratch? Like this?' He demonstrated scratching by crossing his arms and tickling his armpits. Hana laughed and the sound cut through the sudden tension in the group.

It had had even more of an effect on Luke. The way he was looking at Hana now brought a lump to Anahera's throat. She knew how that felt—the unbelievable joy of hearing Hana laugh for the first time. It was something she would never forget. Like the feeling when she'd seen that first smile and witnessed those first, wobbly baby steps.

Luke had missed out on so much and she wanted to make up for it somehow. To share all those things. Would he want to see the baby photos and videos or was it too soon? It might be like rubbing salt into a very raw wound at this point.

'Bessie fixed it,' Hana said. 'She put *magic* stuff on it and it stopped scratching. See?'

Twisting her little body, she pointed to the back of ·

her knee. A small red dot was barely visible. No wonder Anahera hadn't spotted it at bathtime.

She raised her gaze to find Luke watching her and for a long moment they held the eye contact. The telepathic conversation was the kind that only parents would have when they were sharing the same worry about their child.

And it felt...*good*. As if something huge that had been missing from her life was suddenly there.

Someone to share the worry. Coming home to live with her mother had given her that kind of relief but this was different. Her mother was more like an extension of herself. Luke was Hana's father—the missing piece of the puzzle.

'It must have been days ago,' she said aloud. 'It's almost gone.'

I'll be watching her, her gaze added. *Like a hawk. Don't worry...*

'I wonder what the "magic" stuff was,' Sam said. 'Maybe it's an ointment made from the same bushes they make that M'Langi tea from?'

'I'll ask Bessie,' Vailea said. She held out her hand to Hana. 'Come on, darling. I'm going to give you some dinner and then it's time for your bath.'

Luke was still watching even when they had disappeared into the house. He was struggling a bit with how overwhelming this was.

Anyone would have found Hana an adorable child. Listening to her talk, seeing the wonder of life shining from her eyes, hearing her *laugh*... To know that this was his daughter made it so much more powerful. The connection was already there—he could feel it in every cell of his body. The love was there, too, ready to be bestowed, and the need to offer protection was so strong he'd felt a moment of sheer panic when she'd told them about that mosquito bite.

How ridiculous was that? The odds of it having been from an infected mosquito were very low and she was obviously perfectly healthy days after the event. It could have been more than a week ago, in fact, and she could be well past the time when symptoms of encephalitis could appear.

'An ointment is a bit different from tea,' Anahera was saying to Sam. 'Maybe they use a different part of the bush. Like the bark. Don't they use the leaves for the tea?'

'It wouldn't be the bark.' Luke tried to refocus his attention on the conversation. 'I've been doing a bit of reading about the medicinal uses of hibiscus. The tea's usually made from an infusion of the flowers from crimson or magenta-coloured flowers. Leaves can be used, too, but the bark's only useful for making rope or caulking ships.'

'Have you found any scientific evidence of effects?' Sam leaned forward, clearly interested in the subject. Anahera had turned her head to glance at the door to the house. Would she prefer to be inside with her family?

'There's been quite a lot of studies done,' he told Sam. 'There's some evidence that it acts as a mild diuretic and it can lower blood pressure in people with type two diabetes.'

'That could be useful. Type two diabetes is getting to be an increasing problem in all the islands.'

'It can also act as a gentle laxative, apparently. And

an anti-inflammatory. It's supposed to be good for stomach irritation. Some researchers think it may contain chemicals that work like antibiotics.'

'Not so farfetched to think it could work like an antiviral, then?'

'Hmm. I read something about it potentially being able to kill worms so maybe going down the track of an insect repellent is valid.'

It was so much easier having Sam here. For a short time Luke had been so immersed in this discussion he'd been totally distracted from where he was—and why...

But then Hana appeared again and this time she was wearing a pair of pink pyjamas that had a butterfly print on them. Her hair was a mass of damp ringlets and her face was full of the joy of life again.

'Come over here, chicken,' Sam said. 'I want my goodnight kiss.'

Hana happily scrambled over Bugsy and held her arms up for a cuddle. Sam tickled her until she shrieked with laughter and then kissed the top of her head with a loud smack.

'Sweet dreams,' he said.

Hana wriggled out of his arms. Anahera stood up. 'Bedtime, sweetheart,' she said. There was a tiny silence as everybody noticed the little girl wasn't moving. Anahera cleared her throat. 'Don't forget to say goodnight to Luke.'

There was shyness back in those big brown eyes. She'd just been released from a loving farewell from her uncle Sam but this was new ground and she wasn't sure how to say goodnight to this new person in her life. How had Sam made it seem so natural? Oh, yeah... Luke smiled and held out his arms.

He wasn't really expecting Hana to accept the offered hug. Not this easily anyway, but she didn't hesitate. She knew what to do now and those little arms went round his neck and squeezed hard. For just a precious few seconds Luke could feel the whole shape of that little body. He could feel her heart beating and the puff of her breath on his neck.

The feeling of loss when she wriggled free was equally unexpected and Luke found himself blinking hard as he watched Anahera scoop Hana into her arms. She clung like a little monkey, her arms and legs wrapped around her mother, and he could see the way the little body instantly relaxed, her head burrowing into the dip below Anahera's shoulder and her eyes closing. By the look of it, she would probably be asleep by the time she was put into her bed. There was no mistaking the bond between these two as Anahera's head tilted to press against Hana's drying curls. Nobody else existed for either of them in that moment, and Luke felt the exclusion so clearly it was a physical ache. Was it even possible to become a part of that human unit?

Again, he found himself staring at the empty frame of the front door when Anahera had carried Hana inside.

'That went well,' Sam murmured. 'Don't you think?'

Luke didn't respond with anything more than a grunt and he picked up his beer to avoid having to try and articulate what he was thinking.

He wouldn't have known where to start anyway. Instead, he let his gaze drift. To the bowl of petals on the table and then over the railings of the veranda to the village surrounding this small house. The sun was setting but there was a group of children playing football farther down on the dusty road. The faint sound of their laughter could be easily heard.

Could he imagine his daughter living in London? Where would you go to find brightly coloured petals there? Where were there any roads that would be a safe playground?

He couldn't imagine it. Anahera was right—merging their lives would never have worked.

And he'd been right, too. She had never *really* loved him. Okay, he could accept why she'd kept Hana's existence a secret at first but to keep it up when she knew the truth… That was unacceptable. Unthinkable. How could anyone do that to someone they cared about?

Discovering just how much he had missed out on was making it all the worse.

His appetite had fled and he was hard put to do more than taste the delicious meal that Vailea had prepared.

'Must be something in the air,' she said. 'Hana wasn't hungry either.'

'Well, I've made up for them both.' Sam sighed. 'We might need to take the long way home, Bugsy.'

'I'll come with you,' Luke said. 'I'd like to talk about the M'Langi tea study with you some more.'

There was a sudden, awkward silence. And then Vailea reached for his half-empty plate and it sounded like she was deliberately trying to keep her tone casual. 'I thought you and Ana might like a chance to talk,' she said. 'I've got some coffee brewing.'

Anahera was pushing a bit of fish around her plate.

Maybe her appetite hadn't been any better than his own. She looked up, and he was reminded of the moment they'd met, when he'd been horrified to see what had looked like fear in her eyes. How had it come to this—that she could be afraid of him and what he might do to her life?

He couldn't go there now. It would be so hard and he was already emotionally exhausted.

'We'll have plenty of time to talk,' he said. 'Thank you, Vailea. This has been…been…' He couldn't find any words. What had happened here this evening for him was simply too huge.

'It was a pleasure.' Vailea touched his arm before picking up the plate, excusing him from having to say anything more. 'You're welcome here any time, Luke. You're part of our family now.'

Sam must have sensed that this was the best note to end this introduction on. He clicked his fingers to summon Bugsy and hugged both Vailea and Anahera. Maybe Luke was expected to follow suit but it was all suddenly too much. He could only mutter his thanks and duck his head in farewell before following Sam.

'It was a good start,' Sam said. 'You all need a bit of time now to get used to things. You'll work it out.'

'I hope so.'

'You're a lucky man, you know that?'

Luke's breath came out in a huff. 'It's a mess, mate. How come that's lucky?'

'You have the most beautiful daughter on earth. I'd give my right arm for a gift like that.'

They walked in silence for a while, and Luke found the colliding thoughts and feelings in his head beginning to slow down and find a pattern.

A gift.

Yes. Despite the fact that he had lost his trust in Anahera and knew they could never have a future together, their child was a gift that would change his life for ever in a very good way.

He should find happiness in that and he did. Of course he did. It was just unfair that opposing emotions seemed to be two-sided coins. Love and hate. Happiness and sadness. That particular coin seemed to be spinning on its side for him right now. Which side would end up showing? The unimaginable happiness of having Hana in his life?

Or the sadness in losing Ana?

CHAPTER TEN

'I DON'T WANT IT.'

'But mango's your favourite. Would you rather have an egg? With soldiers?'

'No.' Hana rubbed at her eyes with tight little fists, and Anahera cast a worried glance at Vailea, who was almost ready to leave for work. She kissed the cloud of curls in need of brushing and moved towards her mother as she lowered her voice.

'She barely ate anything last night either. And look at her—she looks like she needs to go back to sleep.'

'It's early.' Vailea's smile was reassuring. 'You could both go back to bed for a bit, love. It's your day off, after all.' She picked up her bag. 'If you're worried, bring her up to see Sam later.'

Anahera nodded. She felt Hana's forehead. She put her hand on her own forehead and then felt Hana's again. Was it warmer?

'What are you doing, Mumma?'

'Just checking. Do you feel sick, sweetheart? Have you got a sore throat or a sore head?'

'No.'

'Are you still tired?' Anahera was tired herself, which was hardly surprising after another night of

sleep eluding her. Her mother's suggestion was starting to seem rather attractive. 'Shall we go and have a
cuddle in Mummy's bed for a bit and have a story?'

Hana smiled and nodded and slid off her chair. 'I'll
get my book. The *big* book...'

The worry ebbed. The big book was an illustrated
version of old fairy tales that Hana loved. The day
would soon get too hot to laze in bed but she could
enjoy some time reading aloud with her daughter cud-
dled deliciously under her arm, tiny fingers ready to
help turn the pages and point out the most fascinating
things in the pictures.

Time out. If she was reading aloud, her mind
couldn't wander and fret about Hana's lack of appetite.

Or when they were going to see Luke again.

And what the future might hold...

For a while it was lovely. Hana dozed off, and Anahera soon followed her example. She probably didn't
sleep for more than an hour but it was the uncomfort-
able warmth that woke her. Hana's skin felt hot and
sticky, and a wave of panic washed through her.

'Hana? Wake up, darling.' Her grip must have been
firmer than she realised because Hana woke up with a
start and immediately burst into tears. Anahera pulled
her into a cuddle. 'Oh, I'm sorry...I didn't mean to
give you a fright.'

'Go away, Mumma.' Hana was trying to wriggle
free as her sobs quickly subsided. 'You're too hot...'

She was hot?

Of course she was. The sun was well up and stream-
ing into her bedroom and they'd been lying under the
covers together. She didn't normally panic like that.
What was wrong with her?

'Let's have a shower. We'll pretend we're under the waterfall up by the lagoon.'

That was lovely, too. Hana was smiling under the cool rain of the shower and she even ate a piece of mango afterwards. It was Anahera whose appetite had vanished now.

'Shall we go to the beach and have a swim? Or up to the lagoon?'

Hana shook her head.

'Where would you like to go, then? Or shall we stay at home today?'

'I want to go to the patercillar house.' Big, brown eyes held a pleading edge. 'With Luke.'

Anahera's heart sank.

'But that's in London, sweetheart. It's a long, long way away.'

'I want to go.' There were tears rapidly filling her eyes now and it wouldn't be long before they were rolling down her face. It was so unlike Hana that Anahera was alarmed.

Children could pick up on things that had been left unspoken. Was she unsettled by Luke's appearance in her life without knowing why?

Or was it something more serious? As a medical professional, Anahera knew that a mother's instinct was not something to be ignored.

'Tell you what. Let's go and visit Uncle Sam. He might let us take Bugsy for a walk around the lagoon.'

It was a particularly hot day. The humidity was high and the walk was long and slow. Bone-dry dust coated their feet and geckos basked on the rocks, oblivious to their steps. Even the bright yellow trumpets of the allemande vine looked wilted and maybe it wasn't surprising that Hana was definitely not her usual, chatty self. Anahera didn't want to upset her by trying to force conversation so, for the most part, it was a silent companionship. She frequently found her mind wandering, and every time it logged into the circuitous worry about Luke and the future that was rapidly becoming a well-worn track.

She normally loved her days off and time to spend with her daughter like this but happiness was elusive today. She tried to remember what it felt like to be really happy in the hope that she could turn her mood around in case that was something else that Hana was picking up on.

When had she been the happiest in her life?

That was easy. When Hana had been born and she'd held the miracle that was her new baby in her arms for the first time.

Or maybe it wasn't so easy. Impossible not to also think of the time she had believed she was the happiest it was possible to ever be—when she'd been head over heels in love with Luke Wilson. In that happy bubble that she'd been so careful to protect so that nobody would know and do anything to dim the rainbow shine it had had.

Such different kinds of happiness. Mother love was deep and warm and for ever, but the *in* love one was shinier and amazing. Both had a piercing sweetness, but the mother love was more solid and dependable. Nothing could change that.

Luke had had his first taste of that parent-child bond last night. Was he even more aware of everything he'd missed out on now?

The guilt was still there but it had changed shape.

Now it was about what she had stolen from Luke instead of what she was keeping hidden. Things that she could never give back—like the miracle of Hana's birth and the milestones of her babyhood.

Did he hate her even more?

It hit her like a mental slap that she was doing it again. Making this about herself.

Being selfish.

She couldn't change what she had done, however wrong it had been, but she could try and do the right thing and that was to make up for it in some way, no matter how hard it might be.

She could welcome Luke back into her life as Hana's father and she could share the parenting. Hana would get a daddy who loved her and—if she was lucky—maybe he would eventually forgive her and she would end up with the best friend she could hope for.

It seemed like a big step in moving forward and for a moment Anahera could feel enormous relief. But then her treacherous mind came up with another angle of how it might impact on her. What if Luke got married again and presented Hana with a substitute mother?

Was the thought so shocking it transferred itself through her hand to Hana and made the little girl stumble?

Whatever the cause, Hana was in tears yet again and she had grazed her knee.

'I don't want to walk any more, Mumma. My legs are sleepy.'

'I'll carry you. It's not far now. We'll visit Uncle Sam and then go and see Nana in the kitchen for lunch, okay?'

''Kay...' Still sniffling, Hana let herself be lifted and wrapped her arms around her mother's neck as she settled onto her hip.

Anahera kept walking up the hill but it was even slower going now. When had Hana become so heavy?

The sniffles stopped after a short time and she could feel Hana's body going floppy as the little girl fell asleep, which seemed to make her even heavier. By the time she reached the hospital it was becoming quite a struggle to keep carrying her. Entering the walkway, Anahera headed towards the staffroom, hoping that Sam might be in there for lunch by now, but the only person present was Luke, who had papers spread over the table and was working on a laptop.

'Hi...'

'Hello...' Luke got to his feet. 'I thought this was your day off.'

'It is. I've brought Hana up to see Sam. She's...a bit off colour, I think.'

'In what way?' Luke was close enough to touch Hana within a couple of swift steps. He smoothed back her hair and dipped his head so he could see her face. 'Hey, Hana...what's up?'

Hana moved her head as if the touch was irritating but didn't open her eyes or make any response. Luke's gaze flicked up to meet Anahera's.

'She's barely touched any food and she's...just not herself. She keeps crying and she almost *never* cries...'

Luke had his hand on her forehead now. 'She feels a bit warm.'

'It's pretty hot outside. It was a long walk up the hill.'

'Is she usually this sleepy at this time of day?'

Anahera shook her head. 'She gave up on naps by the time she was eighteen months old.' Oh, help. She could see the shadow that flicked over Luke's face. Sadness that he hadn't known this fact about his own daughter? She had to look away. Had to try and change her grip on Hana, too, because her arms were really aching now with the effort of holding her.

'Let me take her,' Luke said. He matched his words with action and gently scooped her out of Anahera's arms. 'It's probably nothing more than a cold or something coming on but let's go and check her out.'

'Do you know where Sam is?'

'Doing an outpatient clinic.'

'We need to head that way, too. We could use one of the treatment rooms in the emergency department.'

Luke flicked a glance over the mop of curls nestled into his shoulder. 'Would you rather Sam had a look at Hana?'

This was the first chance she'd had to show Luke that she wasn't going to keep him shut out of his daughter's life any more but she didn't get the chance to say anything because Luke answered his own question.

'He probably should. I'm not actually working here and you aren't supposed to treat your own children, are you?'

'But you're the expert,' Anahera said quietly. 'If it is… You know…' She couldn't voice her worst fear that this was, indeed, another terrifying case of the dreaded encephalitis.

'Right now, I feel more like a father than a doctor.' Luke was staring straight ahead now and he spotted the figure in the green uniform first. 'Hey, Hettie?

Could you grab Sam when he has a moment, please? We'll be in the treatment room with Hana. She's not feeling so great.'

'Oh, no!' Hettie was looking worried as they walked closer. 'We're almost done with the clinic. We'll be there in a tick.'

Hana woke up as Luke put her on the bed in the treatment room.

'Hullo, sleepyhead,' he said softly.

Hana just stared up at him. She didn't smile but she didn't burst into tears either. For a long moment they just seemed to stare at each other, and Anahera was sure she'd been right. Whether she was picking up on nonverbal signals or if it was some unexplained genetic connection, Hana knew there was something very important about this new man in her life.

The moment was broken when Sam, closely followed by Hettie, came into the room.

'What's happening?' His glance at Anahera was reassuring and his tone was cheerful as he directed his words at Hana. 'You haven't gone and caught a naughty bug, have you, chicken?'

Hana's head rolled from side to side. 'I'm not naughty.'

'Not you. It's the bug that's naughty if it's making you feel sick.'

'I'm not sick.'

'Good.' Sam's smile was enough to make everyone in the room relax a little. 'You won't mind if I have a look at you to make sure, though, will you? Hettie? Let's get some vital signs.'

'I can do that.' Anahera was already stretching out

her arm to get the tympanic thermometer to check Hana's temperature but Hettie stepped in front of her.

'My job.' She smiled. 'You're the mummy here, remember?'

She was. It was her job to reassure Hana and explain what was happening so she didn't get frightened by any of the tests that Sam might want to include in his examination, and she knew it would be a thorough one because Sam loved Hana and he knew that Anahera wouldn't have brought her in unless she was genuinely worried.

But it seemed that she wasn't needed to keep Hana either distracted or co-operative because Luke was already doing her job.

'Let's get your T-shirt off. That way Uncle Sam can see if you've got any spots—like a butterfly.' He was helping her to pull it over her head. 'Do you like the butterflies with spots the best? I do.'

'I like the yellow ones.'

'What about blue ones? Do you get those really tiny blue ones here like this?' Luke held his thumb and forefinger a centimetre or two apart.

'Temperature's well up,' Hettie reported quietly. 'So's her heart rate.' She wrote on the form, and Anahera had to swallow hard as she watched the clipboard being hung on the end of Hana's bed. Had her daughter just become an official patient?

'I'm going to feel your neck,' Sam said as he checked her lymph nodes after peering down her throat. 'You tell me if it's sore.'

Anahera edged closer to the bed to read the figures Hettie had written on the chart. She should have been able to pick up that Hana had a fever. Or had her temperature spiked during the walk when she'd been so hot herself it had been hard to tell?

'Tummy-tickling time,' Sam announced. 'And then we're going to play with the stethoscope.'

It was certainly a very thorough examination. Anahera could see Luke nodding at some unspoken question that came from Sam and then he started on a neurological assessment, checking strength and sensation and pupil reaction, and all Anahera could do was stand there and wait for the verdict and try—unsuccessfully—not to be reminded of Sam doing all these tests on little Hami when he'd come in with the fever that had been the first sign of his fatal encephalitis.

This small treatment room seemed crowded with people who had all the knowledge in the world that could be needed but it was still possible that they might all be helpless in the face of a disease they couldn't control.

Anahera had never been more scared in her life.

There had been times in his career when Luke had wished there was more he could do for his patients. Times when he felt frustrated—angry, even—like he had when he'd been powerless to save Tane. He'd had patients he'd grown very close to, like Harry, and many that he'd cared about deeply enough to experience memorable joy in their recovery or sadness for their outcomes.

But he'd never, ever felt like this.

Scared…

Hana looked so little and fragile, sitting on a bed that was too large for her, in nothing more than a pair of knickers that had—surprise, surprise—a butter-fly print.

He could see her ribs clearly outlined beneath that perfect olive skin and the wave of protective tender-ness that washed through him was almost unbearable.

He could also see the flushed cheeks of a rising fever and the concern in Sam's gaze as he looked up, still moving the disc of his stethoscope gently over that small chest and back.

'Something's certainly going on,' he said quietly. 'The question is—what?' He took his earpieces out. 'It could just be a cold. Her throat is slightly inflamed and her ears are a bit red. Chest's clear, though, and there's no sign of any rash. Let's get a dose of paracetamol on board and I'll get some bloods off but…'

His raised eyebrow invited Luke's input and he had to say it. 'Given the history of the mosquito bite, a lumbar puncture would tell us what we really want to know.'

Anahera's intake of breath was audible, at least to him. It wasn't a pleasant procedure for parents to watch. He could feel his own gut tightening at the thought of a needle being stuck between those tiny vertebrae he could see protruding from Hana's back as she sat with her little shoulders hunched.

'I can stay with her,' Hettie offered. 'And we'll put a good dollop of anaesthetic cream on now. By the time that's taken effect, it'll be painless.'

She would still have to be held very still and it would be frightening.

'I'm not going anywhere,' Anahera murmured. 'If anyone's going to hold her, it's going to be me.' She took the dose of paracetamol syrup from Hettie's hand.

'Of course it is,' Luke said. He caught Anahera's gaze as she stepped closer to give the medication to Hana and he held it, trying to offer what reassurance he could. Trying to let her know that he was in her corner. That Hana had both her parents here to worry about her. As her gaze clung to his for a heartbeat, and then another, he was aware of a new strength coming from somewhere. Something strong and good. He could do this and he could help. He was helping already because some of that fear was ebbing from Ana's eyes.

'In that case, I'm probably superfluous.' Hettie smiled. 'I might go and get on with some work in the ward, unless...' The glance in Luke's direction was curious but everybody knew he was the encephalitis expert. Of course he'd want to be involved in this case.

'I know my way around a manometer,' he told her. 'I can assist Sam.'

Hettie paused on her way out of the treatment room. 'Want me to get a bed ready?'

'I think so.' Sam nodded. 'We'll want to keep an eye on her for a while yet.'

Hana was intrigued rather than frightened by the application of the topical anaesthetic cream both to her back and the crook of her elbow beneath sticky patches, and her eyelids were drooping noticeably as Anahera gave her a cuddle and then tucked her up with a light sheet as a cover. She was asleep—yet again— almost instantly.

'We'll give it an hour to make sure it's done its thing,' Sam said. 'I might grab a bite of lunch and I'll let Vailea know you're here. Can I bring you a sandwich or something, Ana?'

She shook her head. 'I'm really not hungry.'

'Neither am I,' Luke said. 'We'll just stay here and look after Hana.'

Sam's gaze travelled from him to Hana and then to her mother and back to him. His slow nod suggested that this arrangement was exactly as it should be.

'Come and get me if anything changes. Won't be long.'

Luke arranged chairs on each side of the bed, and they sat with their sleeping child between them.

'I can't believe this is happening,' Anahera whispered.

'Try not to worry. We don't know if it's anything to worry *about* yet.'

'When it's your baby, you worry about everything.'

'Yeah…' Luke's voice cracked. 'I'm discovering that.'

There was a long silence and then Anahera spoke in no more than a whisper. 'I'm sorry, Luke. I'm sorry for everything but most of all that I didn't tell you about Hana. That you've missed so much…'

'I could have gone my whole life not knowing what I *was* missing,' he told her. 'Without knowing what this could feel like. It's… It feels like…a new beginning.'

'I don't blame you for hating me…'

'I don't hate you, Ana.'

It was true. He might not trust her any more and he might be angry that she could have gone as far as to make love with him and still not told him the truth. He might be feeling betrayed and hurt as well, but hate didn't come into it. That coin would never land on that side because he had truly loved her once.

Anahera's head was bent now. Was she trying to hide the fact that she was crying? She reached out to smooth an errant curl that was stuck to Hana's flushed little cheek and as she put it back where it belonged, her hand stayed there, gently cupping her daughter's head.

Luke could feel the strength of that love. A bond that nothing could ever break. He could feel the fear, too.

'It'll be okay,' he murmured. 'I know it will.'

Anahera didn't look up. 'You don't know that.' Her voice was raw. 'We had a little boy come in once, not long after I came back home. His name was Hami and he was the same age as Hana. His mum brought him in because he had a fever and she couldn't wake him up properly and…and…'

'He had encephalitis?'

Anahera nodded. She didn't have to tell him how the case had turned out. He could see the fat tears rolling down her face. He could imagine what it must have been like to have a patient who reminded you of your own child. How devastating it would be to lose the fight. He'd only discovered he was a father yesterday but he knew already that his interaction with paediatric patients would never be the same. He might have thought he understood how precious they were to their parents and how hard it was, but you never really knew, did you, until you walked in their shoes? How amazing that he'd only needed to take a few steps to feel like he'd stepped onto a new planet.

A planet that put a whole new perspective on everything, and there was a downside that was all too obvious now because it gave you new things to be afraid of.

Anahera was afraid. She'd been afraid of *him* when he'd turned up so unexpectedly in her life and he'd felt like a complete jerk because he'd assumed that fear had sprung from how badly he'd hurt her by not telling her the truth about Jane.

But she'd been afraid of losing Hana, hadn't she? Just the way she was now.

He recognised that fear because he could feel it himself. This feeling of needing to protect a vulnerable child might be very new but it was astonishingly powerful. He would do whatever it took to make sure Hana was safe.

Anahera thought she had been protecting Hana by not telling him the truth. Protecting herself, too. Trying to hang on to the safe place she'd thought she'd found for her family.

And hadn't he done exactly the same thing to her?

He hadn't told her about Jane because it would have destroyed the safe place that Wildfire Island had been for him. It would have destroyed the miracle of finding love, which had been the last thing he'd expected.

It hadn't *felt* like lying, though…

He'd been protecting himself. Just the way that Anahera had been.

Luke was staring at Anahera, even though he could only see the top of her head. That shiny, soft black hair that rippled down her back because she wasn't working today and hadn't braided it. His fingers tingled as they reminded him what it felt like to have the weight of that hair slipping through them. She had taken her hand from Hana's head and traced it over the little, bare shoulder and down the arm until she could take her daughter's hand gently in her own. Bowing her head even farther, she lifted Hana's hand to touch it with her lips.

The gesture was so tender it made Luke's heart ache but his head was still grappling with new thoughts that seemed increasingly important. Maybe Anahera had convinced herself she wasn't really lying to him. She had, after all, told him part of the truth.

But she'd made love with him and still hadn't told him.

He'd done the same thing, though, hadn't he? He'd made love with her without telling her anything about Jane. Hana had been conceived on one of those stolen nights. How many opportunities had he had to tell her the truth? Opportunities that had only became impossible to grasp because he'd known that if he had, Anahera would never have allowed that kind of intimacy. He'd wanted—*needed*—it too much to risk that.

But that had been then and this was now.

The destruction of his trust in Anahera ever since he'd learned the truth made the idea of being that close to her seem abhorrent. You couldn't make love with someone you couldn't trust.

His head was spinning. Anahera must have felt like that when she'd lost her trust in *him*. Even if they'd been in the same place, she wouldn't have wanted to talk to him, let alone be close enough to touch.

What had changed?

She must have forgiven him, that was what it was.

And she must have wanted to be with him as much as he had wanted to be with her.

She'd told him that she'd loved him more than she thought it was possible to love anyone.

Had.

Past tense. She'd also said that it was too late.

It was always too late, Luke. We just didn't know it...

'It's *not* too late.'

'What?' Anahera's head came up with a jerk.

Oh, God…had he said that aloud? This wasn't the time or the place to talk about anything in the past or even what could still be between them now. This time was about Hana. Nothing else mattered.

Her face was white. 'Did you say it was *too late*?'

'No…the opposite. I said it's *not* too late.'

'I don't understand…'

Luke was spared having to try and explain by Sam's return. He had Vailea with him, and Hana woke up and then it was time to take a blood sample and get the procedure of the lumbar puncture over with.

The topical anaesthetic on her elbow had made getting that sample relatively painless but it was still frightening for Hana, and when the sticky patch was peeled from her back she knew there was more to come and her co-operation ceased.

'I need you to lie on your side, darling. And curl up.' Anahera was trying to bend Hana's knees and get her bent so that the spaces between her vertebrae were as wide as possible.

'*No-o-o*…I want to go *home*.' Hana pushed at her mother with her arms and kicked her legs, and her sobs were becoming heartbreaking.

Sam was pulling on a pair of sterile gloves and looked at Vailea with a head tilt to ask for her help but the older woman was looking almost as upset as Hana. She had a hand pressed to her mouth and it was shaking visibly.

Luke touched her arm. 'You go,' he said quietly. 'It's not as bad as it looks. And it'll be over soon. I'll come and find you.'

And then he stepped closer to the bed and crouched so that his head was on the same level as Hana's.

'Hana?' He had to raise his voice to cut through her wails and be heard. And he tried to sound as if he had something very exciting to tell her.

It didn't work. So Luke clicked his fingers in front of her face. Then he did it again, above his head.

'What's this, Hana?'

He clicked them again, close to Hana, to one side of her head and then the other. Up high and down low beneath the level of the bed.

'Do you know what it is?'

Hana had stopped crying. She stared at Luke as she rolled her head slowly from one side to the other to say 'no'.

'It's a butterfly,' Luke told her. 'With hiccups.'

The small, miserable face crumpled again, but this time it was with a smile. A sound emerged that could be a giggle.

But laughter could turn to tears very easily.

Luke knew he had only a very small window of time to do something a bit more heroic.

It was the worst thing in the world for a mother to have to restrain her child to allow someone to do something frightening and potentially painful. Anahera couldn't blame her mother for being unable to help or even watch.

This was killing her.

And then Luke stepped in and caught Hana's attention. In the surprising silence that fell, he began talking in a quiet, gentle voice that was utterly compelling.

'You know how butterflies are caterpillars first and then they change?'

Hana didn't say anything or nod but she was clearly listening. The gasping breaths that had fuelled the terrified crying were subsiding into rapid breathing with just the occasional hiccup.

'Did you know they make themselves a little house called a chrysalis so they can hide inside and not come out until they're a real butterfly?'

'A…a patercillar house?'

Luke nodded. 'And you know what? They have to curl up inside that house. Just the way Mummy wants you to curl up now. Could you do that, sweetheart? Could you curl up like a caterpillar?'

It was the first time Anahera had heard him use an endearment for someone other than herself. The first time she had heard that level of caring. Weirdly, it was making *her* feel loved so surely Hana could feel it, too?

She could. The little girl gave an enormous sniff. ''Kay…'

'That's my girl. Caterpillars have lots and lots of legs. How many have you got?'

'Two…'

'That's right.' Luke's smile was genuinely impressed. 'And they curl them up just like that…'

It was easy now to slip her arms into place and rest them on Hana's legs so that she could prevent any movement.

'There's going to be a little bit of rain on top of your chrysalis now,' Luke said. 'Can you feel the cold water dripping on your back?'

Sam had a lopsided smile on his face as he swabbed Hana's back with antiseptic. He was clearly as blown away as Anahera was with how effective the distraction was that Luke was providing.

'There might be a little twig that pushes on you, too. It doesn't hurt, does it? You can just feel it pushing.'

Sam had injected local anaesthetic into deeper tissues through the numbed top layer of skin. Then he slipped the needle into where it needed to be without so much as a whimper or twitch from Hana. Spinal fluid was always so slow to drip into the test tubes but Anahera couldn't believe how fast it was all over.

'You can come out of your chrysalis now, sweetheart.'

'Will I have wings?'

'You sure will. Very soon.'

Anahera widened her eyes. Luke was new to being a parent but surely he knew he shouldn't make promises he couldn't keep?

Not that it mattered. The procedure was over and Hana was happy and it was all thanks to Luke.

She had never loved him more than she did right then. Releasing the gentle hold she'd had on her daughter, she looked up to meet his gaze, and his eyes were as gentle as his tone had been with Hana. The smile that curled his lips was slow and *so* beautiful. The kind of smile she'd never thought she'd receive from him again.

Was it so impossible to believe that he could forgive her?

That, somehow, in the midst of this apparent crisis, he'd done so already?

'I'll go and start testing this.' Sam was collecting up the test tubes. 'She might have a bit of a headache for a while but hopefully the paracetamol she's got on board will deal with that. We'll top up the dose soon.'

The anti-inflammatory did seem to prevent the headache that was a common side effect from having some spinal fluid removed. It seemed to be helping with the fever, too. Hana's cheeks were looking less flushed. She fell asleep again, but this time it seemed less alarming—the sleep of a small child who was worn out by unusual events.

Or was that wishful thinking?

Like Hana growing wings?

'She'll want them,' she warned Luke. 'Those wings you promised her.'

'I wouldn't promise anything I couldn't deliver.'

Anahera's heart skipped a beat at the serious note in his voice. He was giving her a message that had nothing to do with a promise made to a child.

But then he smiled. 'I was playing around online last night, wondering what I could get for Hana for her birthday. I found a pink sparkly fairy outfit that comes with a set of wings. I admit I'm no expert in such things, but it looked to me like fairy wings are pretty much the same as butterfly wings. It should be on the next supply plane that comes out.'

'Oh...' Why on earth had she never thought of that? 'She'll *love* that...'

If she was well enough. A lot could happen in the few days before the next plane was due from the mainland.

It was an opportune moment for Sam to come into the room. He had Vailea with him and her smile made

Anahera catch and hold her breath. Did she already know something? Something good?

'First results look great,' he said. 'Completely normal. I really don't think we're looking at anything more than your average kiddy bug. We'll still keep her in overnight for everybody's peace of mind but I wouldn't be at all surprised if she bounces back to her normal gorgeous self by tomorrow morning.'

Anahera burst into tears and threw herself into Luke's arms.

Or maybe he had pulled her into them.

It didn't matter. They both needed this fierce hug that was a release from the worst fear in the world.

They needed each other.

CHAPTER ELEVEN

'Here. This is the place.'

It was the wooden bench in the hospital's tropical garden where Luke had kissed her as the sun had risen after that long night when Tane had been admitted.

Vailea had been happy to sit with her granddaughter. She'd practically shooed Anahera and Luke out the door of the room when they'd finally stopped hugging each other.

'Go.' She'd smiled. 'Find a quiet place. You two need to talk.'

And Luke had chosen this place. The spot where he'd been able to drag her back in time and make her realise that she'd never stopped loving him.

She never would.

And it felt... It felt like Luke didn't want her to. He had taken her hand as they'd left Hana's room and he still hadn't let it go by the time they sat down on the bench. If anything, he was holding it even more tightly. Looking at her as if there was something of the utmost importance that he wanted to say but was struggling to find the words.

'I'm sorry,' he finally managed. 'You're a better person than I am, Ana.'

'*What?*' Anahera blinked.

'I judged you. I couldn't get my head around how you could have slept with me when you hadn't told me the truth, and then I realised I'd done the same thing to you when I didn't tell you about Jane.'

'But that was a long time ago. And it was me who judged *you*. And I was wrong. I knew that as soon as you told me.'

'And you forgave me, didn't you? Otherwise you wouldn't have… You couldn't have been so…'

He had to be referring to that intense connection between them when they'd made love. Had it only been the night before last? The memory was still fresh enough to bring a flush of colour to Anahera's cheeks and a very noticeable warmth to far more private parts of her body.

She managed a smile. 'Of course not. There's nothing to forgive anyway, because I understand. It was my fault. I should have listened when I had the chance. I—'

Luke's finger on her lips stopped her words.

'And I understand now, too. What it feels like to be a parent. There's nothing for me to forgive either.'

'But you've missed so much…'

'Then let's make sure I don't miss any more. I still love you, Ana. I will never stop loving you. I know you think there's no way to make it work but…but we have to *try*, don't we?'

Anahera nodded as tears filled her eyes. She already knew that she'd been wrong to base assumptions on the tragedy that had been her mother's love story but there would be another time to tell him about that. She had something more important to say.

'I love you, too, Luke. And we'll find a way to make it work. You're right. We have to. For Hana's sake.'

Luke's smile was crooked. 'For my sake, too. I can't imagine my life without you. I want to marry you, Ana. I want to have more children with you. I don't know how we'll do it but I want... Dammit, I want it *all*.'

This time it seemed quite okay to be a bit selfish.

'I want it, too,' Anahera whispered. 'Every bit of it.'

In some ways this kiss was very like the first one they had shared in this very spot. It was inevitable. A reminder of every past touch—every loving gesture.

It was still the feeling of coming home.

But at the same time, it was so much more than the last kiss had been because this time it held a solemn promise of what the future would hold.

And yet Luke was frowning as he finally let Anahera take a proper breath.

'I'll have to go back to London very soon. I'll have to sort out how I'm going to change my job.' He smiled again. 'You know, my senior registrar has been eyeing up my job for years. If I gave him the chance to job-share, I think he'd be over the moon.'

'So you could spend time here on the island as well? That would be perfect.'

But he shook his head. 'Not when I'll have to leave you behind. And Hana, when I'm only starting to get to know her.'

'We could come with you. I'm not going to let you completely sacrifice the life you already have. And certainly not your job. You're doing things that are too important—for people like our islanders, amongst others. You and that friend of yours—Harry? You're going to change a lot of people's lives if this vaccine works.'

'But it's winter in London at the moment. It's cold and grey and…you'd hate it. Hana would hate it.'

'Not if she could go to the patercillar house.'

Luke's smile made the corners of his eyes crinkle in a way Anahera had never seen before and she fell a little bit more in love with him—the way she had when she'd been there to share the way he had calmed and distracted Hana so that what could have been a horrible procedure had become almost a game. And the way he had cared for her mother, making it okay for her to leave when she'd been finding things unbearable.

As if it was an extension of her thoughts, Vailea appeared on the garden path, looking a little tentative as she approached in case she was interrupting something important.

'Hana's awake,' she told them. 'And she really wants an ice cream. I can get one from the kitchen, but I thought you might like to be the ones to give it to her.'

She had to be feeling a lot better if she was asking for ice cream. A smile curled Anahera's lips and then kept growing.

'We can give her something even better to go with that ice cream,' she told her mother. 'We can give her a daddy.'

Luke's sharp intake of breath was an echo of the expression on Vailea's face.

'It's not…too soon to tell her?'

'No.' Anahera caught Luke's hand and stood up, bringing him to his feet as well. 'It's not too soon.'

She was still smiling like the happiest woman in the world as she looked up at the man she loved. 'And you were right. It's not too late either.'

Luke bent his head to kiss her again. 'Let's do it,' he whispered into her hair. 'Let's make a family.'

And that was exactly what they did.

* * * * *

MILLS & BOON®
Hardback – February 2016

ROMANCE

Leonetti's Housekeeper Bride	Lynne Graham
The Surprise De Angelis Baby	Cathy Williams
Castelli's Virgin Widow	Caitlin Crews
The Consequence He Must Claim	Dani Collins
Helios Crowns His Mistress	Michelle Smart
Illicit Night with the Greek	Susanna Carr
The Sheikh's Pregnant Prisoner	Tara Pammi
A Deal Sealed by Passion	Louise Fuller
Saved by the CEO	Barbara Wallace
Pregnant with a Royal Baby!	Susan Meier
A Deal to Mend Their Marriage	Michelle Douglas
Swept into the Rich Man's World	Katrina Cudmore
His Shock Valentine's Proposal	Amy Ruttan
Craving Her Ex-Army Doc	Amy Ruttan
The Man She Could Never Forget	Meredith Webber
The Nurse Who Stole His Heart	Alison Roberts
Her Holiday Miracle	Joanna Neil
Discovering Dr Riley	Annie Claydon
His Forever Family	Sarah M. Anderson
How to Sleep with the Boss	Janice Maynard

MILLS & BOON®
Large Print – February 2016

ROMANCE

Claimed for Makarov's Baby	Sharon Kendrick
An Heir Fit for a King	Abby Green
The Wedding Night Debt	Cathy Williams
Seducing His Enemy's Daughter	Annie West
Reunited for the Billionaire's Legacy	Jennifer Hayward
Hidden in the Sheikh's Harem	Michelle Conder
Resisting the Sicilian Playboy	Amanda Cinelli
Soldier, Hero...Husband?	Cara Colter
Falling for Mr December	Kate Hardy
The Baby Who Saved Christmas	Alison Roberts
A Proposal Worth Millions	Sophie Pembroke

HISTORICAL

Christian Seaton: Duke of Danger	Carole Mortimer
The Soldier's Rebel Lover	Marguerite Kaye
Return of Scandal's Son	Janice Preston
The Forgotten Daughter	Lauri Robinson
No Conventional Miss	Eleanor Webster

MEDICAL

Hot Doc from Her Past	Tina Beckett
Surgeons, Rivals...Lovers	Amalie Berlin
Best Friend to Perfect Bride	Jennifer Taylor
Resisting Her Rebel Doc	Joanna Neil
A Baby to Bind Them	Susanne Hampton
Doctor...to Duchess?	Annie O'Neil

MILLS & BOON®
Hardback – March 2016

ROMANCE

The Italian's Ruthless Seduction	Miranda Lee
Awakened by Her Desert Captor	Abby Green
A Forbidden Temptation	Anne Mather
A Vow to Secure His Legacy	Annie West
Carrying the King's Pride	Jennifer Hayward
Bound to the Tuscan Billionaire	Susan Stephens
Required to Wear the Tycoon's Ring	Maggie Cox
The Secret That Shocked De Santis	Natalie Anderson
The Greek's Ready-Made Wife	Jennifer Faye
Crown Prince's Chosen Bride	Kandy Shepherd
Billionaire, Boss...Bridegroom?	Kate Hardy
Married for their Miracle Baby	Soraya Lane
The Socialite's Secret	Carol Marinelli
London's Most Eligible Doctor	Annie O'Neil
Saving Maddie's Baby	Marion Lennox
A Sheikh to Capture Her Heart	Meredith Webber
Breaking All Their Rules	Sue MacKay
One Life-Changing Night	Louisa Heaton
The CEO's Unexpected Child	Andrea Laurence
Snowbound with the Boss	Maureen Child

MILLS & BOON®
Large Print – March 2016

ROMANCE

A Christmas Vow of Seduction	Maisey Yates
Brazilian's Nine Months' Notice	Susan Stephens
The Sheikh's Christmas Conquest	Sharon Kendrick
Shackled to the Sheikh	Trish Morey
Unwrapping the Castelli Secret	Caitlin Crews
A Marriage Fit for a Sinner	Maya Blake
Larenzo's Christmas Baby	Kate Hewitt
His Lost-and-Found Bride	Scarlet Wilson
Housekeeper Under the Mistletoe	Cara Colter
Gift-Wrapped in Her Wedding Dress	Kandy Shepherd
The Prince's Christmas Vow	Jennifer Faye

HISTORICAL

His Housekeeper's Christmas Wish	Louise Allen
Temptation of a Governess	Sarah Mallory
The Demure Miss Manning	Amanda McCabe
Enticing Benedict Cole	Eliza Redgold
In the King's Service	Margaret Moore

MEDICAL

Falling at the Surgeon's Feet	Lucy Ryder
One Night in New York	Amy Ruttan
Daredevil, Doctor...Husband?	Alison Roberts
The Doctor She'd Never Forget	Annie Claydon
Reunited...in Paris!	Sue MacKay
French Fling to Forever	Karin Baine

MILLS & BOON®

Why shop at millsandboon.co.uk?

Each year, thousands of romance readers find their perfect read at millsandboon.co.uk. That's because we're passionate about bringing you the very best romantic fiction. Here are some of the advantages of shopping at www.millsandboon.co.uk:

* **Get new books first**—you'll be able to buy your favourite books one month before they hit the shops

* **Get exclusive discounts**—you'll also be able to buy our specially created monthly collections, with up to 50% off the RRP

* **Find your favourite authors**—latest news, interviews and new releases for all your favourite authors and series on our website, plus ideas for what to try next

* **Join in**—once you've bought your favourite books, don't forget to register with us to rate, review and join in the discussions

Visit **www.millsandboon.co.uk**
for all this and more today!